Dear Reader,

I just wanted to tell you h
publisher has decided to r
books. Some of them have not been available for a while,
and amongst them there are titles that have often been
requested.

I can't remember a time when I haven't written, although
it was not until my daughter was born that I felt confident
enough to attempt to get anything published. With my
husband's encouragement, my first book was accepted,
and since then there have been over 130 more.

Not that the thrill of having a book published gets
any less. I still feel the same excitement when a new
manuscript is accepted. But it's you, my readers, to
whom I owe so much. Your support—and particularly
your letters—give me so much pleasure.

I hope you enjoy this collection of some of my favorite
novels.

Anne Mather

Back by Popular Demand

With a phenomenal one hundred and thirty-five books published by Harlequin, Anne Mather is one of the world's most popular romance authors. Harlequin is proud to bring back many of these highly sought-after novels in a special Collector's Edition.

Anne MATHER

COLLECTOR'S EDITION

A FEVER IN THE BLOOD

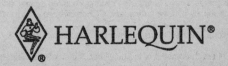

HARLEQUIN®

TORONTO • NEW YORK • LONDON
AMSTERDAM • PARIS • SYDNEY • HAMBURG
STOCKHOLM • ATHENS • TOKYO • MILAN • MADRID
PRAGUE • WARSAW • BUDAPEST • AUCKLAND

ISBN 0-373-63144-8

A FEVER IN THE BLOOD

First North American Publication 1990.

Copyright © 1989 by Anne Mather.

This edition published by arrangement with Harlequin Books S.A.

® and TM are trademarks of the publisher. Trademarks indicated with
® are registered in the United States Patent and Trademark Office, the
Canadian Trade Marks Office and in other countries.

Visit us at www.eHarlequin.com

Printed in U.S.A.

CHAPTER ONE

BEN SCORCESE let himself into his apartment on the Piazza del Fiore with an audible sigh of relief. It was so good to be home, he reflected pleasurably, and he was looking forward to the next six weeks, with nothing more demanding to do than to continue with his manuscript. These last months had been interesting, of course, and he had enjoyed lecturing in both Australia and New Zealand. But his main occupation these days was research, and for weeks he had been promising himself that, once his summer holiday started, he would settle down and try to finish the treatise he was writing.

Dropping his suitcase inside the door, he bent to pick up the half-dozen or so letters that lay waiting for him. Evidently, Signora Cipriani had not expected him back so soon, or the letters would all have been deposited neatly on the desk in his study. It was obvious from the thickness of the dust lying on the table in the narrow hallway, and the faint smell of mustiness in the air, that she had not opened up the apartment for a couple of weeks. The distinctive combination of dry vegetation and compressed heat was unmistakable, and Ben guessed his part-time housekeeper had not overworked herself in his absence.

Closing the heavy door behind him, Ben slung the bag containing the papers he had been studying on the plane, and his camera, down beside his suitcase, and carried his mail through to the kitchen. Before looking at the letters, he opened both of the sash windows that overlooked the yard at the back of the building, breathing the cooler air of early evening with some relief. Below, peach trees were espaliered to the crumbling wall that enclosed the cobbled courtyard, and a huge black cat was sprawled in its shade. There was a timelessness about the scene that appealed to Ben's senses; a feeling of permanence that complemented his mood. For the first time in his life, he felt he was content—and if, very occasionally, he experienced a certain impatience with his own complacency, those moments were becoming fewer and further between.

It was in this mood of happy anticipation that he turned to pick up the letters again from the veined marble worktop where he had dropped them. In spite of the age of the building, the kitchen of the apartment was fairly modern, with a stainless steel sink standing cheek by jowl with a rather ancient cooker. Mrs Cipriani had added colour to the room by furnishing it with dozens of trailing plants, whose greenery, Ben felt, seemed in danger of taking the whole place over. Neglected or not, the plants still flourished, and he pulled a wry face as he propped his lean hips against the drainer.

Most of the letters were either bills, or bank statements, or circulars, and he discarded them without further ado. Whatever utility he had not paid could wait another day at least, and he was about to abandon their perusal in favour of examining the contents of his fridge when a pale cream envelope grabbed his attention. He would have recognised that barely legible scrawl anywhere, even without the fact that the envelope was addressed with only his name: *Signor Benvenuto Scorcese*, and nothing else. Which meant that it had to have been delivered personally, unless Cass had got someone else to deliver it for her.

With an impatience he at once ridiculed and despised, he tore the envelope open, scanning the scalloped cream sheet that emerged with narrow-eyed intensity. It was from Cass; and it had been delivered by hand. She was here, in Florence, and she needed to see him *urgently*.

The date on the letter, he saw, was six days old. Which meant she might not still be in the city. Did she know when he was expected home? Had she spoken to Signora Cipriani? Or had she simply contacted the university? He had no way of knowing, and the chances were that she had abandoned her quest after he had made no effort to contact her.

Ben breathed deeply, and then, with the letter still in his hand, he walked through the creeper-hung arch into his living-room-cum-study. The phone was on his desk and he picked up the receiver at once, cradling it between his shoulder and his ear as he flicked through the directory for the number of the Villa Regina. It was the small hotel Cass had stayed at on a previous visit to the city. It was a long shot, but it was the only one he had, and he dialled the number swiftly, unconsciously offering up a silent prayer that she'd still be there.

He transferred the receiver to his other hand as the number rang out. Once; twice; then the receptionist answered, 'Villa Regina. Can I help you?'

'Yes.' Ben paused. 'Could you tell me, do you have a Signora Cassandra Fielding staying at the hotel? She— er—well, she'll probably be occupying a suite.'

'One moment, *signore.*'

The line went dead as the receptionist went to check the computer, and Ben endeavoured to recover his earlier calm. What price now his mood of complacency? he reflected somewhat irritably. A note from Cassandra, and he was as tense as a violin string.

It seemed to take an inordinately long period of time for the hotel receptionist to find out what he wanted to know. By the time she came back on the line, Ben's long fingers were drumming an impatient tattoo on the scratched surface of his desk, and his previous feeling of well-being had completely dissipated.

'Signora Fielding has been a guest at the hotel, *signore*,' she advised him formally, initially raising and then dashing his hopes. 'But she was checking out today, I believe, and as I've had her paged without any success, I'm afraid she must already have gone.'

'Oh.' Ben's response was flat. He paused a moment, and then added swiftly, 'You don't by any chance have a forwarding address?'

'I'm afraid not, *signore*.'

'Do you know if she was leaving for the airport?' he persisted, mentally calculating the times of the London flights out of the international airport at Pisa, but the receptionist was vague.

'She may have been, *signore*,' she responded, evidently trying to accommodate him, but Ben realised his chances of locating Cass at the international airport in Pisa were slim at best.

'Thank you,' he said at last, the disappointment in his low, attractive voice causing a shiver of regret to attack the girl's spine. 'You've been very helpful.'

With the receiver replaced on its cradle, Ben gave way to an exclamation of frustration. Thrusting his fingers through the thick weight of hair that grew back from his forehead, he raked his scalp in raw impatience. If only, he thought grimly. If only he had got back a day sooner; if only Cass had delayed her departure for twenty-four more hours.

Breathing a resigned sigh, he let his hands fall to his sides. There was no point in indulging in futile wishing. He was here now, and Cass wasn't. Whatever desperate need had brought her to Florence either no longer concerned her or had required immediate action, with or without his involvement. It was unfortunate that he had not been there for her when she'd needed him, but that was the way it was. Maybe it was just as well. His mother would not appreciate him getting involved with Cass again. And he knew from past experience that the less he saw of his father's youngest child, the better. All the same...

Dismissing the pang of bitterness that swept over him at memories too powerful to ignore, he determinedly walked back into the hall to rescue his suitcase. Unpacking first and then a shower, he decided briskly. And then he'd decide about food. One thing was certain: Cass's letter had certainly banished any desire to have an early night.

The water was running in the shower, and he was stripped down to his underpants when he heard the doorbell. Mrs Cipriani, he guessed, expelling a weary groan. No doubt she had observed the lights on in the apartment, and had come to apologise for not preparing for his arrival. A glance in the fridge had revealed its bare shelves, and he had acknowledged his mistake in not advising the housekeeper of the actual date of his return.

Even so, he wished she had waited until tomorrow morning to make her explanation. He was not in the mood for her excuses. Nevertheless, he felt obliged to answer the door; and, thrusting his arms into the sleeves of a dark blue towelling bathrobe and wrapping its folds about his waist, he turned off the taps.

But when he opened the door, his expression a mixture of tolerance and weary resignation, it wasn't Mrs Cipriani who was standing outside. It was Cass herself who confronted him, a maroon leather suitcase and matching vanity propped beside her.

'Oh—Ben!' she exclaimed, swallowing with evident relief. And then, continuing in English, the language of the incredibly beautiful woman his father had married when Ben was fifteen years old, she went on, 'I was afraid it might be your housekeeper. But then I thought, it's late, and surely even housekeepers keep sociable hours these days. Only I've been here so many times during the past few days, and you were never at home. As a matter of fact, I was on my way to the airport when something told me to try one last time—'

She was nervous, Ben could see that, the voluble surge of words serving to warn him she was in a highly emotional state. Besides which, her pale face with its hectic splashes of colour, and the wide, dilated pupils of her eyes were an added indication of her agitation. Trouble, he diagnosed grimly, his heart twisting at the instantaneous response she always aroused in him.

'You'd better come in,' he interrupted her shortly. Stepping forward, he picked up her two cases, and she gave him a quick, anxious smile as she brushed past him into the hallway of the apartment. 'The study,' he prompted when she hesitated and, slamming the door with his heel, he set down the cases again before following her into the velvety darkness of his living-room-cum-study.

The lamps he switched on in passing banished the shadows, and revealed the narrow contours of her body beneath the expensive folds of her cream suede suit. She had lost weight, he noticed instinctively, before dismissing the thought. It was nothing to do with him, he told himself irritably. She had never been particularly voluptuous, for all her Italian ancestry, and since her marriage to Roger Fielding her tall, slim body had fined down to near gauntness.

'You—you don't have anything to drink, do you?' she asked then, surprising him still further, and Ben frowned.

'Coffee, you mean?' he enquired, his dark brows drawn together, and Cass sighed.

'Actually, no. I meant—something stronger,' she admitted, shifting a little awkwardly. 'Um—gin? Vodka? Whisky, even?'

Ben thrust his hands into the pockets of his robe. 'I think I have some brandy,' he remarked coolly. Then, when her nod revealed her acquiescence, he drew a taut breath. 'I'll get it,' he said, and indicated the tapestry-covered sofa beneath the windows. 'Why don't you sit down? I shan't be long.'

But when he came back, carrying the bottle of cognac and two fine Murano glasses, she was still on her feet, standing by the window, her whole attitude one of suppressed trepidation.

'Thanks,' she said, taking with evident eagerness the glass he proffered, steadying it with both hands as he poured a generous measure of the warm amber liquid into it. 'Hmm, lovely,' she added, taking a sip. 'I need this!'

'So it would appear,' observed Ben drily, pouring only a small amount of the brandy into his own glass. 'So— what brings you to Florence?'

Cass shook her head, savouring another mouthful of the cognac. 'Where were you?' she asked, not answering him. 'I've tried everywhere!'

'The university?' he suggested, watching her, and she made a frustrated gesture.

'No. Not there,' she conceded, sighing. 'I—well—I didn't want to involve anyone else, and so many people know us at the university.'

'I see.' Ben was unhelpful, but he couldn't prevent the feeling of resentment that was colouring his mood.

'So where were you?' she exclaimed, gazing at him. Lifting his shoulders, he made a careless gesture.

'Is that important? I was away, lecturing, in Australia and New Zealand. You should have warned me when to expect you—'

'And had you make some excuse not to see me?' she interrupted swiftly. 'Oh, no! I've tried that before, remember?'

Ben bent his head. 'I've never deliberately refused to see you.'

'No,' she conceded bitterly. 'But you have been—how shall I put it?—unavailable?'

Ben's eyes were expressionless as he looked at her. 'I do have a job to do, Cass. I can't take time off just when I feel like it.'

'How convenient!' Her lips twisted. 'Well, I'm here now. Do you mind?'

He sighed. 'Let's not get into a pointless discussion, shall we? Just tell me why you're here, and I'll tell you whether I mind or not. Where's Roger? Is he with you?'

'*No!*'

Her denial was so vehement, Ben could feel the hairs on the back of his neck lift apprehensively.

'No?' he echoed, trying to maintain a casual interest. 'So what is this? A shopping trip?'

'No!'

Once again her denial was swift and passionate, and with a feeling of impending doom Ben swallowed the contents of his glass at a gulp. What now?

'I've left Roger,' she announced after a moment's hesitation. 'And before you start, I should tell you, Daddy doesn't know yet.'

Ben groaned. 'You've left Roger?'

'Yes.'

'Does *he* know?'

'He knows. But he doesn't know where I am.' Cass's tongue circled her lips. 'I've been staying at the Villa Regina. Do you remember it? If Roger's thought of me coming here at all, he'll have tried the Excelsior or the Savoy. He doesn't have your address, in any case, and I doubt he'd ask Daddy for it.'

Ben shook his head. 'And why haven't you told your father?'

'Oh——' Cass spun about on one high heel and walked towards the windows again. With her back to him, she said, 'You know why. He'd never approve of my leaving—he'd never take my side. You know how much he wanted this marriage to work. He'll never understand that it's not going to.'

Ben's fingers tightened round his glass. 'How can you be so sure that it's not?' he demanded, his voice harshened by the strength of his own frustration. What price now his summer sabbatical? How was he going to be able to concentrate on the life and times of Ambroise Giotti, when the sixteenth-century historian was so far removed from the problems of his twentieth-century counterpart?

Cass turned then, emptying her glass as she did so. The slender column of her throat was absurdly vulnerable in the lamplight, the silvery lightness of her hair haloed by the pale illumination. He knew she was twenty-two now, but she didn't look it. In the flattering shadows, she looked no more than eighteen. *Eighteen!* His lips tightened. He didn't want to think about Cass at eighteen.

'Are you shocked?' she asked now, once again avoiding his question, and Ben found himself needing another drink.

'May I?' she asked, coming up behind him as he grimly poured himself more brandy, and Ben took her glass with evident disapproval, and splashed a little of the cognac into the bottom.

'Since when have you been hitting the bottle?' he enquired tautly, as she took the glass back from him, and she shrugged. 'Don't tell me Roger has driven you to drink, because I simply won't believe it.'

'Why not?'

Much to his discomfort, she did not open the gap between them once again, but remained where she was, so close that he could smell the elusive perfume she was wearing. It was disturbing and disconcerting, and in spite of his professed maturity it was Ben who felt momentarily threatened. It was a definite effort to withstand her cool appraisal, and he swallowed a mouthful of the brandy before making any response.

'You forget,' he said at last. 'I know Roger. He's not the type to—intimidate anyone.'

Cass regarded him steadily, the wide grey eyes full of reproach. 'You think not?'

Ben groaned. 'Cass, it's a fact! Roger may be Father's tool, but he's no sledge-hammer!' His lips twisted. 'A gavel, perhaps.'

Her jaw jutted. 'And what if I told you there was someone else?'

Ben's heart juddered. 'You—you've fallen in love with someone else?' he asked in a strangled voice, and she gazed at him impatiently.

'Not me, Ben! *Roger!*' She ran slender fingers through the silvery fall of silky straight hair that framed her pale face. 'Roger's got a mistress. A woman he's been seeing for the last six months. Oh—he doesn't know I know, and to begin with I thought I could live with it. But I can't.

It's too humiliating. And I had to get away before Daddy found out.'

Ben scarcely noticed the ominous implication of her final statement. He was still absorbing his relief at discovering that Cass herself was not involved with some other man. Roger, he had learned to live with; but someone else, someone more masculine, more demanding...

'Did you hear what I said?'

Cass was speaking again, and Ben made an effort to marshal his thoughts. 'What? Oh—yes; yes, I heard you,' he acknowledged, taking a deep breath. 'So—you came to me. Why? What do you expect me to do? Play the heavy father myself?'

'You?' For the first time since she had entered the apartment and caused him such an emotional upheaval, Cass allowed a faint smile to touch her lips. 'Oh, Ben,' she exclaimed, and to his dismay she reached up to rub her soft cheek against his roughened jaw. 'Darling, I've never thought of you as a father figure. You know that.' She pulled a rueful face. 'That's really what all this is about, isn't it?' And when he didn't answer, she added, 'I came to you because you're the only person I could come to. I—I need some time to decide what I'm going to do. Time to get my life into some sort of perspective.'

'You can't stay here!'

Ben's denial was instinctive, born as much of a need to protect himself as any altruistic desire to repair her marriage. But she couldn't stay at the apartment. There simply wasn't room.

'I knew you'd say that.' Cass raised her glass to her lips and drained it once again. 'As you've always refused to let me stay here, I doubted any circumstances—no matter how desperate—would persuade you to change your mind,' she finished bitterly.

'Cass—'

'Anyway, it doesn't matter,' she continued, taking the brandy bottle from him and pouring herself another. 'I didn't expect you to say I could stay here. No,' she paused, slanting a considering grey gaze up at him, 'I want you to ask your mother if I can stay at the villa for the summer.'

Ben blinked. 'Are you serious?' He shook his head. He could imagine his mother's reaction to that suggestion.

'Why not?' Cass regarded him defensively. 'I have stayed at the villa before. Lots of times, you know that. We used to stay there together before—'

'Things are different now,' Ben interrupted her harshly, swallowing the dregs of his own brandy without enjoyment, and Cass sniffed.

'I know that, too. I know Sophia blamed me for what happened, and she was probably right. But that was years ago now. I'm not the same person, and I don't suppose she is. Won't you at least ask her? If you won't, I don't know what I'll do.'

This last was said with a real note of desperation in her voice, and Ben's nerves clenched. 'What is that supposed to mean?' he demanded, grasping her arm and swinging her round to face him, and then wished he hadn't when the haunting appeal of her expression tore into his gut.

'What do you think it means?' she retorted after a moment, pulling her arm out of his grasp and pressing it protectively against her side. 'Oh, don't worry, I'm not threatening to kill myself or anything melodramatic like that. You won't have my death on your conscience, if that's what you're afraid of. I—I just thought you might help me, that's all. You—you are my brother, aren't you? You used to say you cared what happened to me.'

'I do care,' grated Ben through his teeth, and then, taking a hoarse breath, he turned away. 'All right, all right, I'll speak to her,' he conceded. 'But I can't promise anything. You have to understand that.'

'Oh, I do. I do!' The relief in Cass's voice was almost palpable, and the little laugh she gave was triumphant. 'Oh, Ben,' she cried, 'I knew I could depend on you. You won't let me down.'

Ben wished he could feel as confident. In the twenty or so minutes since he had let her into the apartment, Cass had systematically destroyed the whole fabric of a life it had taken him years to construct. He had thought he was secure; inviolate; no longer vulnerable to the demands of the secular world. Safe within the walls of his academic fortress, he had foolishly imagined that nothing could penetrate its protected façade, but he had been wrong. And now he had to live with that knowledge as well as everything else.

'Have you eaten?' Cass asked suddenly, and he forced his mind into less traumatic channels.

'Eaten?'

'Well, you have just got back, haven't you? Isn't that what you said?' Cass was shedding her jacket as she spoke, revealing the narrow bones of her shoulders exposed by the tan silk vest she was wearing underneath. She wasn't wearing a bra, and he averted his eyes from the small breasts pressing pointedly against the thin material. She was so thin, he thought again, reluctantly anguished by the admission. Dear heaven, what had been happening to her? Whatever it was, he couldn't let it go on.

Now he brushed back his hair with a weary hand and glanced down at his bathrobe. 'Well,' he said, striving for normality, 'I was going to take a shower. Mrs C. didn't expect me back today, and as she hasn't stocked the fridge, I was going to go out for something to eat.' That wasn't actually true. He had decided to go straight to bed, but he couldn't tell her that.

Cass lifted her shoulders. 'Go out?' she repeated, without much enthusiasm. Then, 'Is that little shop still open? You know—the one just off the *piazza*?'

Ben frowned. 'How do you know about that?'

Cass grimaced. 'Well—as a matter of fact, I went in there yesterday afternoon. I thought—oh, I just thought they might know where you were.'

Ben's mouth turned down. 'And?'

Cass made a defensive gesture. 'They didn't.' She met his dark gaze defiantly. 'Don't look like that. I was desperate. I've told you.' She paused. 'Well? Are they still open?'

Ben hesitated. 'They might be.'

'Good. Then I'll go and buy us some food. I can prepare it while you're having your shower, hmm?'

Ben was torn two ways. On the one hand was the fairly urgent desire to get her out of his apartment forthwith, and on the other a reluctant understanding of her reasons for wanting to eat here. After all, it was summer in Italy; the height of the tourist season. Anyone could see Cass and report her whereabouts to either their father or Roger. And while that might, conceivably, be the safest solution, it was not one Ben could live with. Not tonight, anyway.

But thinking of Guido Scorcese reminded him of something else, something he had forgotten until now. 'Why did you say you had to get away before Father found out about Roger?' he asked abruptly. 'What does he have to do with it?'

'Oh…' Cass shifted a little uncomfortably now. 'You know.'

'No, I don't.'

'You must.' Cass spread her arms. 'Daddy must have told you.'

'Told me what?' There was an edge to Ben's voice now. 'I should remind you, our father is not prone to confide in me.'

'No, but—oh!' Cass sighed, and then, apparently deciding he was serious, she said, 'Daddy would expect me to confide in him. As—as I did before.'

'Before?' Ben gazed at her disbelievingly. 'This has happened before?'

Cass swallowed. 'Just once,' she admitted unhappily, and he swore colourfully in his own language. 'I think it was the same woman, actually.'

'The bastard!' he muttered, reverting back to English. 'And what happened then?'

Cass lifted her slim shoulders. 'Daddy—talked to him.'

'Threatened him, you mean.'

'Something like that.' Cass bent her head. 'Anyway, he—Daddy, that is—persuaded Roger to stay. But I don't want that!' she burst out tremulously. 'I don't want Roger to try and make our marriage work just because he's afraid Daddy's going to cut him out of the company. You don't know how that makes me feel.'

'I can guess,' said Ben quietly, and, compelled by a force stronger than himself, he reached out and took her quivering shoulders between his hands, pulling her convulsively towards him.

She came into his arms willingly, her slim body feeling almost fragile against the solidity of his. Her arms slid round his waist, and she pressed her face against his chest, and presently a warm wetness penetrated the parted lapels of his robe, revealing she was in tears.

'Hey!' he exclaimed, his own voice suspiciously thick as he found her chin with one hand and tilted her face up to his. 'Don't cry. No one's going to force you to go back to him. Not as long as I'm here.'

'Oh, Ben!' Her voice quivered. 'What would I do without you?'

Ben steeled himself against the impulse to lick the salty pearls of her tears from her cheeks, and gently but firmly put her away from him. 'Well, that's not a question you're going to have to answer,' he replied, speaking with determined brightness. 'And to answer your earlier question: yes, the shop you mentioned will still be open. Will you make the meal, or shall I?'

'I will,' she answered at once, smudging away her tears with a slightly unsteady finger. 'We'll have meat and *fettuccine* and some of that lovely mozzarella cheese, hmm?'

'All right.' Ben nodded. 'Do you need any money?'

Cass pulled a face. 'It's my treat.' She paused, and then offered awkwardly, 'About tonight. You're not going to send me back to the Regina, are you?'

Ben succeeded in concealing his real reactions to that. 'No,' he told her evenly. 'No, of course not. You can stay here. But I'd advise you not to tell my mother. She might not understand.'

CHAPTER TWO

CASS shifted restlessly beneath the light quilt, wondering if Ben was having as much of a problem in sleeping as she was. Probably, she decided, remembering the narrowness of the spare bed, and her own guilt when he'd insisted she use his room. Although, as he had just returned from Australia and New Zealand, he was probably tired enough to sleep on a clothes-line.

She, on the other hand, had had little enough to do during the last few days but hide out in her hotel room, waiting anxiously to see if Ben returned to his apartment. She had thought of going to the university, but the idea of her own personal problems becoming the subject of speculation among the other members of the teaching fraternity had persuaded her against it. And for the same reason she had avoided approaching Mrs Cipriani. The little Italian woman was a very likeable character, but she was inclined to gossip. And until Ben came back, Cass had not wanted any spy of Roger's, or her father's, discovering her whereabouts from her.

The decision to come to the apartment one last time on her way to the airport had been an inspiration, as it happened. When she had seen the lights burning in the apartment her heart had almost stopped beating, and, trusting that it was too late for Mrs Cipriani to be working, she had dismissed her cab and entered the building.

She sighed. It had been so good to see Ben again. She had missed him so much since her marriage to Roger, particularly as Ben never visited London these days. In-

21

deed, he seemed to have lost all interest in her, she reflected disconsolately. Ever since that last disastrous summer at Calvado, he had avoided her like the plague.

She sighed, shifting on to her back and shading her eyes against the moonlight streaming through the slats in the blind. If only it was possible to turn back the clock, she thought unhappily. She would make sure nothing happened to spoil the relationship they had once had.

She sighed again. When she was growing up, Ben had been a regular visitor to the house in Eaton Chare. Even the feud, which had existed between Sophia and Guido ever since her father had divorced Ben's mother and married again, had not turned Ben against them. He had even gone to university in London, and Cass knew her father had expected him to make his home in England. The head office of the lucrative Scorcese shipping empire was there, and Guido had naturally assumed Ben would join the family business.

But he hadn't. Cass grimaced now, remembering the rows he and her father had had when Ben had unexpectedly decided that he wanted to teach. She had been too young to understand, of course, but she could remember being afraid even then that Ben might stay away.

But her fears had been unfounded. Ben had stayed on in England until she was twelve, taking a doctorate in medieval history. And, even when he gave in to his mother's pleas and got an appointment at the university in Florence to be nearer her, there were still the long holidays when they could see one another.

She remembered she had been fourteen the first year Ben had invited her to spend a few weeks with him and his mother in Italy. Sophia Scorcese's villa at Calvado, on the Ligurian coast just south of Genoa, was in an idyllic position, and, although Cass had never quite worked out how Ben had persuaded his mother to let her stay, she had had a marvellous time. It had been the first of several such holidays and, if her own mother had never been entirely enthusiastic about the arrangement, her father had encouraged the liaison. Perhaps he had hoped she might persuade Ben to change his mind about joining the company. Whatever the reason, she had been only too happy to go, and, determined socialite that she was, Diana Scorcese had been easily diverted from family problems. As a child, Cass had fondly imagined it had been her mother's ability to arrange parties and look beautiful that had caused her father to fall out of love with his first wife and into love with Diana. It was only as she got older she had learned that Guido's marriage to Sophia had been over long before he met Diana. The Italian woman from a small village in Tuscany, whom he had been obliged to marry because she was carrying his son, had never wanted to share the success her husband had created. Sophia was not a socialite; she had never wanted to leave Italy. And when Guido had transferred his headquarters from Genoa to London, their marriage had been virtually over.

Cass supposed she could understand Sophia's resentment at her son's friendship with the daughter of that second marriage. It must have been pretty galling for her having to accept Cass into her home, even if she had been little more than a child to begin with. After all, she was the daughter of the woman who had forced Guido to abandon his religious beliefs and divorce his first wife. Until Diana came along, their separation had not defied any of the laws of the Catholic Church, and Sophia had been reasonably content. However, Diana had wanted more than a sexual commitment, and Guido had wasted no time in acquiring his decree absolute.

Cass remembered her first weeks at Calvado had been

fraught with innuendo. But it had not lasted. Once Sophia had seen how happy they were together, she had had to concede defeat, and until the summer Cass was eighteen, Sophia had borne the girl's company with a mixture of tolerance and resignation. Ben relaxed more when Cass was around, and his mother liked that. Besides, it enabled her to spend more time with him than she might otherwise have done. Sophia had known it was unlikely that Ben would have spent weeks at Calvado if Cass had not been there; and as she had always worried about his getting involved with some unsuitable female, she had acknowledged the advantages of him spending the long vacation entertaining his sister.

Until... Until that fateful summer when she came of age, thought Cass now, rolling on to her stomach and trying to find a cool spot on her pillow. How had it happened? How could she have become so involved with Ben that she had forgotten who he was? It all seemed so unbelievable seen from this distance, and yet wasn't she still turning to Ben because he was the only person in the world who really cared about her?

She buried her hot face in the pillow, trying not to think about Ben, trying to come to terms with her own problems. And the most significant of them was Roger, and what she was going to do about their marriage.

She desperately wished she had never laid eyes on Roger. And she most definitely wished she had never married him. She doubted she would have, had it not been for what had happened at Calvado, but she had rushed off to Bermuda afterwards in a state of some distraction, and he had been there, waiting for her.

Of course, her mother had wanted to know why she had chosen to join them, after all; why she had come back from Italy weeks before she had been expected; and Roger had provided a convenient excuse. She had met him several months before in London. He was one of her father's blue-eyed boys, a young man of impeccable pedigree, who had accepted her parents' invitation to the villa they owned near Hamilton because he had expected her to be there.

And he had been quite good fun to begin with. He had obviously found her incredibly attractive, which was very satisfying after what had happened, and Cass had behaved with an uncharacteristic abandon—brought on, she suspected, by a kind of defensive defiance.

However, the upshot of letting Roger make love to her one night after a particularly riotous beach party they had attended had resulted in him proposing, and she had accepted, rather foolishly as it turned out.

Of course, her father had been delighted. Denied a son willing to follow in his footsteps, he had adopted Roger as a surrogate, and for the past four years Cass had been desperately trying to make the marriage work. But the truth was, she had little or no interest in their physical relationship, and even though she would have liked to have become pregnant, if only to please her father, it simply hadn't happened. In consequence, they rowed a lot— Roger could be quite horrible when he had been drinking—and he persistently taunted her with his sexual exploits. It was not a recipe for any kind of a life, and Cass knew she had come to the end of her tether. That was why she had done the unforgivable and come to Ben. He had seemed the only person she could turn to. Her mother had always been too busy with her own life to pay much attention to her daughter, and her father—her father would never understand.

She thought now how fortunate she had been in finding Ben at the apartment at last. She had never dreamt he might be away on a lecture tour, or she would certainly not have hung about in Florence, waiting for him to return. Her imagination had only stretched as far as Rome or Genoa, or perhaps to the villa at Calvado. But instead he had been half a world away in the antipodes and, if she had understood his reference to Mrs Cipriani, he had arrived back sooner than he had expected. Another coincidence? she wondered restlessly. Or had she somehow communicated her need of him on a level far beyond their understanding? Whatever the answer might be, he had come back and he had promised to help her; and she ought to be satisfied with that instead of mulling over what might have been...

The smell of freshly brewed coffee awakened her the next morning. It came drifting through her door, which was standing ajar, its pungent aroma a distinct incitement to get up. Cass, who hadn't slept until the early hours, felt little reluctance about getting up. For the first time in months she was looking forward to the day ahead, and, pushing back the quilt, she swung her slender legs out of bed.

The cream satin wrap that matched the nightgown she had unpacked the night before was lying at the foot of the bed; sliding her arms into the sleeves, she got to her feet. Glancing round the bedroom as she did so, she felt a warming feeling of anticipation. Although it was at least four years since she had stayed at the apartment, it was all so wonderfully familiar. It was like coming home, she reflected ruefully, realising Ben might not appreciate her feelings. But that didn't change the way she felt, and she ran her fingers along the brass rail at the foot of the bed as she walked to the door, loving the polished smoothness of the metal beneath her hand.

As she had expected, Ben was in the kitchen, and he looked up somewhat dourly at her entrance. Like her, he was still not dressed, but she guessed from the terseness of his expression that her occupancy of his bedroom was the real reason he was still in his bathrobe.

'Good morning,' she said, refusing to be daunted by his evident disapproval of her attire. 'Oh, isn't it a beautiful day?'

And it was. Ben had opened the windows in the kitchen, and the sun-soaked air was heady with the scent of the flowers that grew in the walled courtyard below. In the tourist haunts of the city there would already be crowds of people, thronging the steps of the Duomo, and snapping their cameras in the Uffizi Museum. But here, in this peaceful backwater, it was possible to enjoy the real Florence, where the moss-covered walls of private villas opened on to quiet squares and *piazzas*. It was the Florence Ben had shown her when she'd first come to Italy, and although she had seen the sculptures in the National Museum, and marvelled at the works of Michelangelo and Brunelleschi, she much preferred his conception of the city.

'Did you sleep well?' Ben asked now, pushing an earthenware mug of strong black coffee towards her, and she smiled her thanks.

'Reasonably,' she lied, wondering if he could tell from the lines around her eyes that she wasn't exactly being honest with him. 'Did you? I'm sure you can't have done on that narrow divan.'

'I've slept in worse places,' he retorted drily, pouring himself another cup of the aromatic beverage. He paused and then added, half reluctantly she felt, 'How do you feel? Had any second thoughts?'

'About staying in Italy, you mean?' Cass perched on

one of the tall bamboo stools that served the breakfast bar. She raised the mug of coffee to her lips and looked at him over the rim. 'No. Did you hope I would?'

Ben gave her a guarded look. 'No,' he replied, after a moment. 'No, I didn't *hope* you would. I just thought you might, that's all. After all, you've had time to think it over. You might have changed your mind.'

Cass put the mug of coffee down. 'I've been here almost a week, Ben,' she reminded him. 'If I'd been going to change my mind, don't you think I'd have done so before now?'

Ben shrugged. 'Not necessarily. You've been in Italy a week, that's true, but until last night you hadn't committed yourself to staying.'

Cass sighed. 'You think I should go back, don't you?'

'Did I say that?'

'You don't have to.' Cass got up from the stool and walked blindly across to the window, wrapping her arms around her waist and staring down into the yard below without really seeing it. 'You've decided you don't want the responsibility. OK. I'll make some other arrangement. But I'm not going back to Roger and that's—'

'I haven't suggested you should,' Ben interrupted her sharply, halting her emotional outburst. 'Stop jumping to conclusions that haven't been reached. I just want you to be sure you know what you're doing. I don't want—I don't want Father blaming me for the break-up of your marriage.'

Cass swung round to face him, hoping her eyes did not look as sore as they felt. 'He wouldn't do that!'

'He might,' retorted Ben flatly. And then, 'Oh, what the hell! He's never approved of anything I've done, so why break the habit of a lifetime?' He took a deep breath. 'If you don't mind, I'll go and take a shower and get dressed. If I'm driving to Calvado later today, I'd better get moving. I've got to see Victor Amorini first.'

Cass clasped her hands together. 'Calvado!' she echoed, feeling a renewed sense of optimism. 'Oh, I can't wait to see the villa again—and the sea!' She lifted her slim shoulders. 'I remember, it was so blue.'

'Yes. Well—' Ben halted in the doorway, his expression revealing his dissension with her words. 'I don't think it's a good idea for you to accompany me to the coast. Not today, at least.' He made a rueful gesture. 'Try and understand.'

Cass straightened her spine. 'You mean, you don't think your mother will allow me to stay,' she declared unevenly. 'Why don't you say so?'

'Hey, what is this?' Ben rolled his eyes towards the ceiling. 'I've told you I'll do what I can to persuade her to let you stay. But you have to give me a little space, too. I can't just turn up at the Villa Andrea with you in tow, and expect Sophia to welcome you with open arms. I need to speak to my mother. I need to explain the situation. Then I'll tell you whether she's prepared to let you stay. And not until.'

Cass bent her head. 'All right.'

'You do believe me, don't you?' Ben made a move as if to come back to her, and then seemed to think better of it. 'Cass, I meant what I said last night. I'm not going to force you to go back to England. Just give me a little time. That's all I ask.'

Cass lifted her head again. 'You—you could telephone,' she ventured, but Ben shook his head.

'It's better if I go and see her,' he replied. 'Remember, I've been away for the past two months. She'll be expecting me to see her when I get back.'

Cass hesitated a moment, and then nodded. 'Yes,' she

said at last. 'You're probably right. But—what do I do in the meantime?'

'You can stay here,' replied Ben at once. 'I should be back tomorrow. I dare say I could make the round trip in a day, if it weren't for having to report in at the university, but it's probably best if I stay the night. She'll expect it.'

'Will she?' Cass half envied his mother. Sophia had the right to demand his time and his attention. She, on the other hand, was a continuing source of nuisance in his life. She wondered what he really thought about her.

'I'll get dressed,' Ben declared now, evidently deciding her question did not require an answer, and after he had gone Cass resumed her seat and finished her mug of coffee.

Not unnaturally, her mind turned to Ben's mother again as she allowed her thoughts to drift. It was almost exactly four years since she had seen her, for although she had occasionally seen Ben in the years between, Sophia Scorcese seldom left her home in Calvado. Cass remembered her as a rather dour woman, lacking in humour, who only seemed to come to life in Ben's presence. That she loved her son, there could be no doubt. That she had ever loved Ben's father was another matter altogether.

Not that Cass had ever seen her father and Ben's mother together. Apart from herself and Ben, the two halves of Guido Scorcese's life had never intermingled. Ben had aunts and uncles and cousins that Cass had never even met, and she knew her own mother's family disregarded her husband's Italian connections.

Getting up again, Cass went to the sink and rinsed out the two beakers she and Ben had used. Then, glancing round, she considered what she was going to do today. The apartment needed cleaning and, although household chores had seldom appealed to her, the idea of cleaning

Ben's apartment was not unattractive. She could do some shopping, too. The fridge needed stocking, and she could buy some food at the little *bottega*. There were one or two personal items she needed as well, and if she stayed away from the city centre no one was likely to recognise her. Of course, there was always the possibility that Mrs Cipriani might appear and resent the fact that Cass was taking over her duties. But, as Ben had said she didn't expect him back so soon, it might be several days before she put in an appearance.

The decision made, Cass left the kitchen and went into the bedroom again, without giving any thought to the fact that Ben might still be in there. In consequence, she came in through the door just as Ben was emerging from the bathroom, his only attire a dark blue towel slotted about his waist.

'Get out of here!' he snarled in his own language, briefly stung into an instinctive response that was both angry and frustrated, and Cass's eyes mirrored her confusion.

'All right, all right, I'm going,' she retorted indignantly, backing out of the door, but as she walked into his living-room-cum-study her confidence wilted a little. Perhaps she ought not to have come here, after all, she thought uneasily, pressing the palms of her hands together and touching the tips of her fingers to her lips. Ben obviously didn't want her here, whatever he said to the contrary, and the idea that Sophia might relent and let her stay at the villa was fast becoming a pointless proposition. She should have stayed in London, and faced her father with the truth: that she and Roger had never had a real marriage, and there was no possible likelihood of them ever producing the grandchildren he wanted so badly.

A sound behind her alerted her to Ben's presence, and she turned to face him rather awkwardly.

'I'm sorry—' she began.

However, his, 'I didn't upset you, did I?' overrode her words, and they both shook their heads a little wryly as the apologies were made.

'I never thought,' added Cass ruefully, and Ben was swift to reassure her.

'It was my fault,' he said, pressing down the collar of his shirt, and wiping a droplet of water from the corner of his jaw. His hair was still damp from his shower, its darkness enhanced by its wetness, and because it needed cutting it tended to curl at his nape. Cass couldn't help thinking how attractive he was with his dark skin and dark eyes, and not for the first time she wondered why he had never got married himself. There had been plenty of women, she remembered, only too willing to show themselves as being attracted to him, and she also remembered how jealous she had been when Sophia had played matchmaker on her son's behalf.

But that was all in the past now, she reminded herself hurriedly, as alarm bells began to echo in her brain. She wasn't here to torment herself with how attractive Ben was, or how foolish she had been all those years ago. She was a grown woman now. She had four years of marriage and a great many daunting experiences behind her. Ben was going to help her, and she had no intention of spoiling things by behaving like a fool.

'I shouldn't have barged in like that,' she insisted now, making a determined effort to behave normally. She watched as he picked up his briefcase and examined its contents. 'When are you leaving?'

'How about now?' responded Ben, snapping the locks on the case again and straightening from his desk. 'If I get to the university before nine-thirty, I'll be able to have a word with Amorini before his ten o'clock lecture.'

'Oh.' Cass swallowed her disappointment, and nodded. Then, 'Yes. Yes, I suppose the sooner you get moving, the sooner you'll be back.'

Ben inclined his head. 'That's what I thought.'

Cass took a breath, her tongue circling her lips. 'Do I— do I say good luck?' she asked, attempting for humour and not really succeeding.

'Just goodbye,' advised Ben drily, picking up the brief-case and looking towards the door. He paused. 'I should get back about lunch time tomorrow. Will you be OK?'

Cass pulled a face. 'And if I say no?' she suggested half jokingly, determined not to let him see how the prospect of another day on her own really affected her, and Ben's eyes narrowed.

'Cass—'

'I'm only teasing!' she exclaimed, not sure that she could cope if he should choose to be sympathetic, and his face cleared.

'OK.' He smiled and her heart turned over. 'If you should need to get in touch with me, the number's in the book by the phone. Do you have enough money?'

'That's one thing that's never been in short supply,' Cass replied swiftly. She hesitated. 'You will drive carefully, won't you? She frowned. 'I suppose you still have that awful sports car?'

'I don't think the technicians at Porsche would agree with you about its being awful, but yes, I'm afraid I still drive a fast car.' He grimaced. 'And you, I suppose, are still afraid of speed. You know, that's one thing I had forgotten about you.'

Cass caught her breath. 'The only thing?' she asked,

unable to prevent the question, and his mouth drew down at the corners.

'I think so,' he replied, holding her gaze for a long, fateful minute. And then, without another word, he went out of the door, and presently she heard the outer door slam as he left the apartment.

CHAPTER THREE

FLORENCE was not a large city, but it was not the easiest place to get out of. Its narrow lanes and one-way streets made driving not only a hazard but a trial, and Ben got heartily sick of having to step on his brakes every time some careless pedestrian stepped negligently into the road.

Yet, for all that, he loved the place, its spectacular blend of ancient and modern as familiar to him as it had been to Dante in his day. There was always something new to see: a shrine glimpsed through an open gateway, the courtyard of a *palazzo* bright with tubs of geraniums. The centuries-old fortresses and Renaissance mansions all jostled cheek by jowl beside the muddy waters of the Arno, whose broad embankments protected the city from the flooding that used to occur.

Ben passed the Ponte Vecchio and headed north-west out of the city, the powerful little Porsche the ideal vehicle to thread in and out of the traffic. The car, which he had bought more than five years ago, remained his one real indulgence, and he had missed its responsive roar and swift acceleration in the rather sedate saloon he had been supplied with during the time he was in Australia.

He remembered now how horrified Cass had been when he had taken her out in the Porsche for the first time. He had driven on to the *autostrada* and given the car its head, and when the speedometer had reached two hundred kilometres an hour she had clutched his arm in a vice-like grip and begged him to slow down. Of course, he hadn't. He hadn't really realised how scared she actually was. He

35

had even laughed; but when he had looked at her and seen her white skin and frozen features he had quickly come to his senses. He had pulled off the motorway and attempted to apologise, to comfort her, but she had lost her head. She had been like a little tigress, he remembered unwillingly, beating at him with her fists until he had been forced to get out of the car and leave her. He had known that, if he had stayed where he was, he might have been tempted to subdue her in a way that would have been totally unforgivable. As it was, when he got into the car again, she had been red-eyed and silent, and for the remainder of the day he had not been able to get a word out of her.

Of course, it hadn't lasted. Cass had never been able to sustain her anger for long. But the car had remained a bone of contention between them, and he wondered if she remembered that day as vividly as he did.

He frowned then, turning his mind away from avenues that were best left unexplored. For the present, he had more immediate problems to confront, not least how best to approach the suggestion of Cass spending the summer at the Villa Andrea. It was not going to be easy, he knew that. For the past four years Cass's name had seldom, if ever, passed his mother's lips. Yet wasn't it a sign of Cass's innocence that she had not hesitated before coming to him—and his mother—for help?

His mouth compressed. Perhaps. But would Sophia see it that way? After all, she was still full of hatred for the man who had divorced her in favour of a younger woman. It didn't matter to Sophia that for years she and Guido had been living apart. He had still been her husband, and she had fought tooth and nail to prevent him gaining his freedom.

Ben sighed as the sleek little sports car slotted in to the

traffic heading for Lucca. It wasn't as if she had loved Guido Scorcese, he thought impatiently. She had only married him because she was pregnant. Yet, for all that, she had been jealous of his second wife: jealous of her youth and sophistication, and most particularly jealous of the daughter he had sired within ten months of their wedding. She had never liked Cass, he remembered reluctantly. Cass had been *that woman's* daughter; a bastard in Sophia's eyes, who regarded marriage as sacrosanct. No matter what had gone before, taking her vows in the church of the Madonna in Genoa had made Sophia Martini Guido Scorcese's partner for life, and nothing and no one could persuade her otherwise.

Ben's hands tightened on the wheel as he steered the car into the fast lane of the *autostrada*. So, he conceded once again, it was not going to be easy to convince his mother that she had to allow Cass to spend the next couple of months at Calvado. Apart from anything else, she would see the break-up of Cass's marriage as proof that nothing good came of going against the will of God. Like father, like daughter, he reflected, anticipating his mother's reaction. She would never accept that it was possible to make a mistake, in marriage as in everything else. And he knew, without a shadow of a doubt, that Sophia would be suspicious of his motives, too, regardless of any claims to the contrary.

Beyond Lucca, the *autostrada* linked with the main route to Genoa, and, glancing at the thin gold watch on his wrist, Ben saw that it was already after one o'clock. He was tempted to stop somewhere and have something to eat, but he suppressed the notion. He knew that idea was simply his subconscious struggling to find reasons to delay his arrival, and although he could have done with a beer he kept his foot on the accelerator.

Calvado was just north of Sestri. It was a charming little
fishing village, overlooking the Bay of Porto Camagio,
that in recent years had become something of a mecca for
yachtsmen. Narrow streets sloped steeply down to the har-
bour, where a new marina provided berths for more glam-
orous craft than the fishing-boats that thronged the jetty,
and one or two good hotels had been converted from the
eighteenth-century residences once used by patrician Gen-
oese families. Gardens, bright with floral displays, nestled
among groves of palm and citrus trees, and from the road
that ran down into the village Ben glimpsed the sandy
cove where he and Cass used to swim and snorkel all
those years ago. Happily, those holidaymakers who found
their way to Calvado had not ruined its character or its
atmosphere, and, had his mother been more amenable to
his continued state of bachelorhood, Ben thought he
would have spent much of his free time at the villa. Not
that Sophia would have approved of any female he might
choose, he reflected wryly. But she persistently produced
so-called 'suitable' young women for his inspection,
daughters of friends of hers for the most part, in whom
Ben had absolutely no interest.

The Villa Andrea was situated on the cliffs overlooking
the bay. Sophia had moved here after her divorce from
Guido Scorcese, preferring the anonymity of Calvado to
the sympathy she would have received from her relatives
in Tuscany. Besides which, there were no reminders of
her husband at Calvado, and although she had made few
friends Ben knew she was not lonely.

The villa was reached down a winding track, where
bushes of crimson oleander sprang up between the gnarled
trunks of ancient olive trees. He passed other villas, whose
gardens were vividly framed against the dark green of the
wooded hillside, and then there was the Villa Andrea,

with its jasmine-strewn walls and morning glory cascading over the porch.

He parked the Porsche in the shade of a clump of citrus trees that had been planted to shelter the villa from the northern winds that blew down from the Alps in winter. Then, leaving his briefcase and the overnight bag he had brought with him in the back of the car, he opened his door and got out.

The view was magnificent. Beyond the cliffs, the deep blue waters of the Ligurian Sea stretched smoothly towards the horizon, dotted here and there with the masts of ocean-going vessels, and the smaller, less spectacular, sails of dinghies. Immediately below the cliffs was the sandy inlet he had glimpsed earlier, while curving round on either side were the lushly vegetated promontories enclosing the Bay of Porto Camagio. He could even see the walls of the Benedictine abbey that stood in splendid seclusion above the town of Porto Camagio itself, and he took a deep, almost reassuring, breath, relishing these moments of personal isolation.

'Benvenuto!'

The sound of his mother's voice—only she ever called him Benvenuto—destroyed his pleasant mood of introspection. For a moment, he almost resented having to abandon the tranquillity of his thoughts to face the argument which he was sure was to come. But then common sense and his own innate sense of decency triumphed over the brief feeling of irritation that had gripped him, and he went to greet his mother with a smile of real affection.

'Mamma,' he murmured gently, as her eager arms enfolded him. *'Come stai, cara? Tu stai bene?'*

Sophia acknowledged his greeting in few words, framing his face in her hands and staring at him as if she expected to see some significant change in his appearance;

Ben found himself growing tense. It was ridiculous, he knew, but it was almost as if she knew there was more to this visit than a reunion after his trip abroad. Yet what could she know? Was he so transparent?

'You look tired,' she said at last, speaking in the Tuscan dialect, which she had always maintained was the purest Italian of all. 'I think this lecture tour you made in Australia and New Zealand has been more arduous than you expected.' Her dark eyes, so like his own, narrowed. 'Or is some woman to blame for this weariness I sense in you?'

Ben released his breath, not without some relief. 'The tour was—exhausting,' he agreed, drawing back from her clinging fingers, and adopting what he hoped was a rueful expression. 'It's good to be back home. I'm looking forward to the rest.'

Sophia's eyes widened. 'You are going to stay?'

Ben cursed his careless tongue. 'I—didn't say that, exactly,' he temporised quickly, glancing back towards the car and then deciding to leave the cases until later. 'Um—I could do with a long, cool drink right now. I didn't stop for lunch, and I'm feeling rather thirsty.'

'Of course.'

Sophia gave him a last considering look before leading the way into the villa. For the moment she was diverted, but Ben knew better than to think his mother would forget his clumsy denial.

The villa, which Guido had bought for her, was much larger than had been needed for one woman and a boy. The spacious rooms, with their cool tiled floors, were elegantly furnished—more elegantly furnished than the house Ben remembered living in in Genoa—and he had often wondered whether Sophia's plan had been to compete in some way with Guido's new home in London.

Certainly, the four bedroom suites, each with its own dressing-room and luxurious bathroom, were not what she had been used to before her marriage. The village she had come from in Tuscany, and where Ben's grandmother still lived, was a simple place, where life continued as it had done for generations. In many ways, Ben envied his so-called 'poor' relations, despite his mother's contempt for them. His cousins might have no ambition, as Sophia frequently declared, but at least they were happy. They had no doubts about their future, and there had never been any conflict of loyalties, such as Ben had lived with all his life.

Now Ben paused in the side hallway, looking about him with genuine appreciation. Whatever reason Sophia had had for demanding such luxurious surroundings for herself and her son, she certainly kept the place in immaculate order. The dark red tiles beneath his feet reflected the polished wood of the balcony above his head, and beyond an arched doorway the wide expanse of the living-room gleamed with a similar lustre. Of course, his mother did not live here entirely alone. She employed a married couple of her own age to do the housekeeping and keep the garden in good order. But Sophia did most of the cooking—even if Maria was expected to clear up afterwards—and when Ben was home she invariably looked after him herself. She maintained that she enjoyed keeping his room tidy and ironing his shirts, and if Ben had any objections he was wise enough to keep them to himself.

The villa itself sprawled over half an acre, with most of its rooms on the ground floor. However, two of the bedrooms were upstairs, and Ben reflected that Cass could have one of those, as she had done before, should his mother agree to let her stay. His own suite of rooms, like Sophia's, was on the ground floor, while attached to the main building by a walkway was a small apartment where Maria and Carlo Alvaro lived.

Maria Alvaro was in the kitchen with his mother when Ben decided to join them. A small, grey-haired woman in her middle fifties, she looked much older than Sophia, who was tall, like her son, and whose long black hair was only lightly touched with age. She was bustling about, setting a tray to Sophia's directions, but she looked up when Ben appeared, and her smile was warmly welcoming.

'It is good to have you back, *signore*,' she greeted him timidly, always slightly in awe of her employer. 'You look well. The Australian air must have agreed with you.'

Ben grinned, but Sophia tutted impatiently. 'He does not look well, he looks weary,' she contradicted the housekeeper sharply. 'But do not worry, Maria. I intend to see that he rests for at least a part of the summer.'

Ben's mouth turned down at the corners, but rather than enter into an argument there and then he went forward and helped himself to a beer from the tray. Eschewing the glass his mother would have pressed on him, he pulled the tab and released a bubbling froth of icy liquid. 'Nectar!' he groaned, raising the can to his lips, and Sophia watched impotently as he quickly drained its contents.

'You should have waited on the terrace,' she declared at last, as he wiped his mouth with the back of his hand. 'Are these the habits you have learned while you are away? To drink beer from a can and use your hand as a napkin?'

Ben grimaced, and ignored the comment. 'Did you cook this ham?' he asked instead, filching a thin slice before she could prevent him, though she slapped his wrist. 'Hmm, it's delicious! Forget I asked the question.'

'Do you think I would buy ham already cooked?' His

mother snorted. 'No, please, I insist you go and sit down.
A kitchen is not the place for a man, and you are getting
under Maria's feet.'

The startled look the housekeeper gave him was eloquent with her surprise at this remark, but Ben decided to
leave them to it. It had always been a source of some
irritation to Sophia that he could look after himself as well
as he did. In her opinion, instead of acquiring an apartment in Florence, he ought to have bought a house; that
way, she could have divided her time between there and
Calvado, making herself the mistress of both dwellings
instead of only the one.

Leaving the singularly modern environs of the kitchen,
Ben crossed the hall again and entered the main *salone*,
or the living-room. Here the colour scheme was light and
restful, with soft velvet sofas, patterned in cream and lime
green, and colour-washed walls framing delicately tex-
tured paintings. Sophia never professed to being an expert,
but she did enjoy having works of art around her, and as
well as the paintings there were several pieces of sculp-
ture, some of them clearly unique, and others—in Ben's
opinion—quite repulsive.

Long windows opened on to a railed terrace that provided a magnificent view of the bay. At this hour of the
afternoon it was bathed in sunlight, and Ben sought the
shelter offered by a shady hammock and, propping his
arms behind his head, determinedly tried to relax. But it
wasn't easy. His mind persisted in dwelling on the reasons
that had brought him to Calvado, and no matter how he
tried, Cass's image as he had last seen her would not be
dislodged.

When Sophia eventually appeared, she was carrying the
tray herself, and Ben quickly stirred himself to draw a
white-painted wrought-iron table towards him. 'Hmm,

thanks,' he murmured dutifully, as she set the meal in front of him, surveying the generous slices of cured ham with fresh melon, the bowl of tossed salad, and the dish of fresh strawberries, with the required air of enthusiasm. There was a bottle of wine, too, a white Chianti, cooled to perfection, a subtle reminder that his mother preferred her drinks out of a glass.

'Go ahead,' she said, when he gave her a questioning glance. 'I have already eaten. If you had had the presence of mind to forewarn me of your arrival, naturally I would have waited. But as you did not...'

Sophia spread an expressive hand as the sentence tailed away, and Ben knew it was yet another pointer to his own shortcomings. Not exactly the most auspicious beginning to his mission, he thought ruefully. But how could he have rung his mother without mentioning the reasons for his visit? No, he had needed to see Sophia, to gauge her reactions for himself.

Despite the fact that he had only had a cup of coffee for breakfast, Ben found his appetite dwindling. It had been different, snatching a slice of ham in the kitchen, drinking beer because he was thirsty. Now, with the most immediate of his hungers appeased, food had become of little importance, and with Sophia watching his every move he was eventually forced to put his fork aside.

'I'm sorry,' he said, aware of her disapproval. 'I think I must be too hot to eat.'

'Too hot? Or too much on edge?' suggested Sophia shrewdly, and Ben pushed the table to one side and sprawled resignedly on the cushions.

'Why should you think I'm on edge?' he responded obliquely. 'I have just driven over two hundred kilometres. Is it so unreasonable that I should feel hot—and tired?'

'No.' His mother, who had seated herself on one of the wrought-iron chairs, crossed her legs and shook her head. 'But you forget, Benvenuto, I have known you for almost thirty-seven years! Credit me with knowing when something is on your mind.'

Ben reached forward and poured himself another glass of Chianti. At least he had no trouble in swallowing the wine, he reflected. And perhaps it would help to loosen his tongue. Right now, he hadn't the faintest idea how he was going to broach the subject of Cass.

'It is a woman, is it not?' Sophia was evidently growing tired of his reticence. 'Who is she? Some Australian woman you met in Melbourne or Sydney? Or is she from New Zealand? What is she? A *Protestant*?' The way she said the word made this supposition intolerable. From Sophia's point of view there could hardly be a worse possibility, except perhaps a *married* woman. And Cass was both.

Ben emptied his glass and decided there was no virtue in procrastination. Whenever he said it—and sooner or later he had to—his mother was going to feel betrayed. She would see Cass's plea for help as a sign of weakness, and she was not likely to agree to his request without a struggle. Of course, he held the ultimate weapon, he knew that, and if all else failed he would use it. But he didn't want to put that kind of pressure on her, though his hopes of doing otherwise were fading fast.

'As a matter of fact, it's Cass,' he said abruptly, and he saw his mother's face suffuse with colour. 'She's here, in Italy.' He paused. 'She's left Roger.'

As if she couldn't sit still under the weight of such news, Sophia got to her feet then, stepping across to the rail of the balcony and gripping the iron with white-knuckled hands. For a moment she just stared at the view, keeping whatever thoughts she had to herself. And then she gave him a sideways glance. 'She has left her husband?'

Ben sighed. 'That's what I said.'

'Why?'

He lifted his broad shoulders. 'That's their business, I suppose.'

'But she told you,' declared his mother harshly. 'Oh, yes, she told you.' Her lips twisted. 'What has happened? Is there some other man? Has her husband found her out in some indiscretion—'

'It's not Cass's fault,' retorted Ben tersely, not prepared to listen to Sophia's distortions of the truth. 'In any case, why she left Roger isn't important. What is important is that she came to us—'

'To you, you mean!'

'—and I've agreed to help her.'

Sophia turned then. 'Help her?' she echoed. 'How can you help her?' Her hands clenched. 'You have no money!'

'I'm not exactly destitute,' said Ben quietly, getting to his feet and pushing his hands into the pockets of his dark trousers. 'In any case, it's not money she needs. It's practical assistance.'

'And what form does this *practical assistance* take?' demanded Sophia contemptuously. 'Does she need a knight in shining armour? A champion to fight her cause?'

'Don't be ridiculous!' Ben was impatient.

'Ah! So I am ridiculous now!' Sophia's eyes flashed. 'But not so ridiculous that I do not see how easily she wraps you round her little finger.'

'That's not true—'

'It *is* true!' Sophia seethed. 'I do not forget that but for her, you would not have chosen to reject the inheritance that would surely have been yours—'

'How I choose to live my life is not in question here,' Ben broke in wearily, trying to keep his temper and not totally succeeding. 'For heaven's sake, Mother, have some pity! The girl's hurt, confused; she needs time and space to come to terms with her feelings.'

'Her feelings?' Sophia snorted. 'And what about my feelings? How am I supposed to feel when you tell me that this woman—this bastard of Guido's—deserves your sympathy but I do not?'

'I didn't say that.'

'But you give little thought to my feelings, none the less,' retorted his mother emotively. 'So—what are you saying? Are you telling me you are going to allow that woman—that *Jezebel*—to stay at your apartment? Are you warning me to keep away? Away from my own son's home?'

This was proving harder than even Ben had anticipated. For heaven's sake, he thought frustratedly, was she being deliberately obtuse?

'No,' he said now, watching a tiny lizard make its way up the wall of the villa. 'No, Cass can't stay at my apartment.'

'At last, you see sense!' Sophia raised expressive eyes to the heavens.

'I want you to let her stay at the villa,' continued Ben flatly, realising there was no other way of saying it. Ignoring his mother's horrified face, he went on, 'You have plenty of room, and she won't need to worry about her father coming bullying her here.'

'You cannot mean this!' As soon as he had finished speaking, Sophia made her outburst. 'Benvenuto, you cannot expect me to take that girl into my house again. I did it once, and look what happened!'

Ben met her gaze steadily. 'That was a long time ago,

Mother. Things have changed. Cass has changed. She's been married for almost four years, remember? She's not a girl any more.'

'There is bad blood in that family,' retorted Sophia bitterly. 'How can you even think of getting involved in this affair? The woman has left her husband; that is what you said, is it not? How do you know she is not lying when she claims it is not her fault that their marriage is not working?'

Ben wondered what his mother would say if he told her he knew because Cass was incapable of lying to him? That he was so closely attuned to her subconscious self, he had known immediately that she had been hurt. But thinking of Cass brought her image vividly to mind, and he averted his eyes so that Sophia should not perceive the anguish it evoked. He had not liked leaving her in Florence, but he had really had no alternative, and he could only hope Roger did not have the nerve to appeal to her father for his address. The idea of Cass's husband turning up at the apartment in his absence filled him with a bitter sense of fury, and the inclination to turn the Porsche around and drive back to Florence tonight was almost an overwhelming temptation.

Now, determinedly putting such thoughts aside, he said quietly, 'Whatever you think about Cass, believe me when I say she would not have come to—me—for help, if she hadn't been desperate.'

'*Desperate?*' His mother was scathing.

'Yes, desperate,' repeated Ben evenly, refusing to be drawn. 'There was no one else she could turn to.'

'What about *her* mother?'

Ben sighed. 'You know what Diana is like.'

'Do I?'

'All right. Point taken.' Ben endeavoured to remain

cool. 'Well, how shall I put it? Diana doesn't like—problems.'

'Who does?'

'No one, but—oh!' Ben raked long fingers through his dark hair. 'Suffice it to say, she would not be sympathetic.'

Sophia regarded him broodingly. 'And this does not arouse your suspicions? That both Guido and her mother refuse to help her?'

Ben groaned. 'They haven't *refused* to help her. For the simple reason that she hasn't asked them.'

'Why not?'

'Oh, *hell*!'

'*Benvenuto!*'

'Well!' He paced grimly across the terrace. Then, turning to look at her again, he scowled. 'Did you turn to your parents when you were in trouble?' he demanded angrily. 'Did you go to *Nonna* and tell her what had happened?'

Now his mother looked away. 'That has nothing to do with it,' she declared stiffly. 'And we said we would not speak of that again.'

'Maybe we have to,' Ben retorted, taking a steadying breath. 'If it's the only way—'

'Cassandra,' said Sophia slowly, evidently loath to use her name, but compelled to do so anyway, 'she is not pregnant, is she?'

Ben felt as though someone had thumped him in the stomach. Pregnant? he thought bleakly. He hadn't thought of that! Was that why she had needed this time alone? Because she knew that she was pregnant, and there was no way she could hide *that*?

Shaking his head, as much to clear his brain as anything, he hid his consternation behind an air of impatience. 'Of course not,' he exclaimed, as if he knew for certain there was no truth in the statement. 'She just needs a breathing space, that's all.'

'So why did she not buy herself a breathing space elsewhere?' his mother countered harshly. 'As you say, money is not in short supply. She could have moved into an hotel, or leased herself a house or an apartment. Instead of burdening you with her problems.'

'Perhaps I don't regard it as a burden,' replied Ben tersely. 'And she needed—*needs*—support, not criticism.'

Sophia's nostrils flared. 'And you expect me to let her come and stay here without asking any questions, is that it?'

Ben bent his head. 'What questions are there to ask?'

'Well, I could ask what your reaction was when she came to you. She did come to you, did she not? Which means you have been writing to her while you were away, while I received only a postcard.'

'Oh, lord!' Ben stared at her now. 'Yes, she came to me, but no, I haven't been writing to her while I've been away. I haven't been writing to anyone. It was just good fortune that I happened to get back a few days earlier than I expected.'

'And you expect me to believe that?'

'Quite frankly, I could care less what you believe,' responded Ben angrily. 'It's the truth. Why would I lie?'

'Why, indeed?' His mother's lips twisted. 'So—where is she now?'

Ben hesitated. 'In Florence.'

'At your apartment?'

'At my apartment, yes.'

'I knew it.' Sophia threw up her hands in frustration.

'Well? Will you allow her to come here?' Ben was not prepared to rise to any more remarks of that kind, and

Sophia's fingers went to the ruffled bow that held the neckline of her cream silk blouse in place.

'And if I say no?'

Ben expelled his breath tiredly. 'Don't make me say it, Mother.'

Sophia's dark brows descended. 'Very well. As I apparently have no choice in the matter, you must do as you see fit. I cannot stop you.'

Ben felt utterly weary. 'I didn't want it to be like this—'

'Well, what did you expect? That I would welcome her with open arms? Do not forget, Benvenuto, she is still that woman's daughter. Aside from anything else, that alone does not endear her to me.'

'I know, I know.' Ben reflected how little exaltation he felt at his victory. 'Well—thank you.'

'Do not thank me!' His mother almost hissed the words. Then, squaring her shoulders, she visibly gathered her composure. 'So—let us not speak of this any longer. It is almost nine weeks since I last saw you, and we have much to talk about. I want to hear about your trip; about the people you met, and about your success in this field. Do you think they will invite you again?'

Ben resisted for a moment, and then, deciding she did indeed deserve to hear about his journey, he sank back on to the swinging hammock. He couldn't go back to Florence tonight, no matter how anxious he might be to do so, so he might as well relax. After all, he did still love his mother, whatever complications she had created in his life.

CHAPTER FOUR

AFTER Ben had gone, Cass made an effort to pull herself together. But it wasn't easy. Despite her earlier determination to fill the day with activity, it was inordinately difficult to find any motivation after Ben's departure. It was even an effort to drag herself into the bathroom and step into the shower cubicle Ben had so recently vacated, and she found herself wiping a smear of soap from the tiles and gazing at it in absent fascination. The cubicle was still warm from its previous occupancy, and she sank back against the wall without turning on the jets. She felt utterly bereft of either energy or enthusiasm, and all she really felt like doing was crawling back into bed.

Eventually she did summon up the strength to turn on the taps, and the force of the water on her sensitised skin brought its own relief. With a return of resolution, she lifted the soap and massaged her languid body until it turned pink beneath her hands, attacking her breasts and her hips and her thighs with a thoroughness born of desperation. She had to be decisive; she had to assert herself. However difficult it was going to prove, she had to show Ben she could be independent.

And, in spite of her morning blues, Cass got through the day without flagging. Mrs Cipriani did not appear, and she was able to dust the furniture and vacuum the rugs without any interruption. She wasn't very experienced when it came to housework, but she made a valiant effort, satisfied with the results she had achieved when she saw the polished wood gleam. She did spend rather longer over tidying Ben's desk than she need have, but the distinctive script of his handwriting caused her no little sense of upheaval. It reminded her of when she was at school and he had written to her, of how anxiously she had waited for the post to be distributed, and how disappointed she had been if he had been late in replying to her letters. Looking back, there seemed no period in her life of which he had not been an integral part—except these years of her marriage, which had been so miserably unhappy.

In the late afternoon, after making do with only another cup of coffee for her lunch, Cass left the apartment. The little *bottega*, that smelled deliciously of the cooked meats and cheeses it sold, wasn't far, and she spent a very satisfying half-hour choosing an assortment of foods to store in the refrigerator. She bought veal and ham and eggs, and several different cheeses, as well as bread and fruit and vegetables, and two more bottles of wine.

However, with the food put away, she was at a loose end again, and she tried to summon up some enthusiasm over what she was going to eat for supper. But the idea of preparing a meal for herself was not appealing, and she eventually decided to make herself a cheese sandwich, and leave anything more ambitious until Ben got back. *Ben...*

Biting her lip, she trudged wearily into the living-room, flinging herself down on the tapestry-covered sofa and trying not to think about what she would do if he should fail in his mission. She *needed* this time in Italy. She needed to get away from London, Roger and her father, and Italy had always seemed to be her spiritual home. She was half-Italian, after all. She wasn't really like her mother at all. A marriage that was only half a marriage could never satisfy the Italian side of her nature. But what she really wanted, she didn't really know—or perhaps she was afraid of finding out...

The telephone rang as she was helping herself to another glass of Ben's brandy. The sudden jangle of sound in the still room was startling, and her hand shook, sending droplets of cognac splashing on to the carpet. 'Damn!' she exclaimed, setting down the bottle and searching futilely for a tissue, but her mind wasn't really on what she was doing. Who was calling? she wondered anxiously. Should she answer it? Oh, what if it was Roger, or her father?

The ringing went on, a jarring counterpoint to her thoughts, and unable to stand it any longer Cass snatched the receiver off its rest. '*Sì?*' she said tautly, wondering if she could get away with pretending to be the housekeeper, and then sank down weakly on to the corner of Ben's desk as his familiar voice sounded in her ear.

'Where the hell were you?'

'Oh, Ben!' She felt so enervated suddenly, she could hardly answer him. 'It's *you.*'

'Who did you expect?' he retorted. And then, 'Oh, of course. You thought it might be Roger.'

'It crossed my mind,' she admitted in a low voice. She took a steadying breath. 'But it's so good to hear your voice.'

'Why?' He was immediately on edge. 'There's nothing wrong?'

'No. No.' She shook her head a little dazedly. 'Nothing's wrong here.' She paused. 'How about you? Did you have a good journey?'

'Reasonably.' His tone was a little clipped now, she thought. 'Are you sure you're all right?'

'Of course.' Cass couldn't ask the question, but it was inherent in her words. 'Is—is your mother well?'

'She's agreed to let you stay, if that's what you mean,' replied Ben a little tersely, and Cass's pulse-rate quickened with sudden relief. 'I'll be back, as I said, about lunch time tomorrow. Could you be ready to leave the day after that?'

So soon! Cass almost said the words, but somehow she managed to restrain herself. It was what she wanted, wasn't it? What she had come here for. Just because she was beginning to feel at home in Ben's apartment was no reason to feel any doubts about her decision.

'Of course,' she said now, forcing a note of enthusiasm into her voice. She paused. 'Are you sure she doesn't mind?'

'You know Sophia,' responded Ben obliquely. 'It's not always easy to know what she thinks. So—if you're sure you're all right, I'll see you tomorrow, hmm?'

'OK.' Cass clung to the phone, wishing she could think of something to delay his ringing off. 'Um—you will drive carefully, won't you?'

'I got here, didn't I?' remarked Ben drily. 'And I always drive carefully. Just because someone not a million miles from where you are is nervous of a little healthy speed...'

'Speed is not healthy,' she retorted, rising to his bait automatically. Then, 'Oh—you!' She had to smile, and the smile coloured her voice. 'Well, until tomorrow, then.'

'*A domani,*' he echoed softly, and she waited until he had replaced his receiver before doing the same with her own.

Of course, she slept badly. Apart from anything else, the amount of coffee she had drunk during the day, combined with the fact that she had eaten very little, had created a build-up of caffeine inside her and her system was unbearably stimulated. Besides which, she had the prospect of meeting Ben's mother again on her mind. Although he had said Sophia had agreed to let her stay at Calvado, Cass was still apprehensive of the kind of welcome she would get. Had Sophia forgiven her? Was she prepared to forget about the past and begin again? Somehow, she doubted it. Sophia had never struck her as a forgiving kind of woman.

So why did she want to go there? she asked herself frustratedly, trying to pound the pillow into some shape that would give her head comfort. Because only at Calvado had she ever been really happy, she acknowledged tiredly. Only with Ben had she ever felt really alive.

She was up again soon after six, leaning out of the kitchen window, trying to catch a little of the promise of the day. At this hour of the morning the sky was tinted a delicate shade of lemon, with gossamer threads of cloud floating like gauze on the calm air. The air itself was still fairly cool, and her breasts hardened into peaks as the thin satin of her nightgown was pressed against them by the breeze. But it was so good to feel in control of her life again, so good to feel free. She hadn't realised how trapped she had felt until she got away.

As she drank her first cup of coffee of the day, a huge black cat stalked along the wall of the courtyard below her, casting a haughty look in her direction. She wondered with some amusement if she had disturbed him in some early-morning tryst, but she felt no sense of blame for doing so. The sun rising over the distant rooftops, the scent of rosemary and verbena, even the aromatic taste of freshly ground coffee, were all serving to lift her spirits, and she determined that nothing, and no one, would spoil her mood.

Before taking her shower, she took a moment to study her reflection in the mirror doors of Ben's closet. The mirrors were old and stained a pale yellow with age, but they didn't prevent her from seeing how thin and pale she had become. At eighteen she had been, if anything, a little plump, with no hollows anywhere and a rounded appearance she had had to struggle to control. Now every bone in her body was barely covered with flesh, and the shadows they created gave her frame a delicate fragility. There were hollows now: in the necklace of bones at her throat, in the framework of her ribs, and in the flatness of her stomach. Even the downy curve of her back exposed every bump in her spine, and the sharp protrusion of her pelvic bones drew attention to the narrowness of her thighs. She looked awful, she thought miserably. She looked as if she was suffering from some wasting illness, and she couldn't imagine what Ben must have thought when he saw her. That he hadn't said anything was typical of him, but that didn't alter the fact that something had to be done to improve things.

And first on her agenda was food, she thought later that morning, after taking a stimulating shower and washing her hair. With her damp hair secured on top of her head with combs, and her narrow limbs concealed beneath a pair of worn jeans and a sloppy T-shirt, she acknowledged that it was many months since she had faced eating with any enthusiasm, but she actually felt hungry now and she was determined to act on it.

Two eggs, whipped into an omelette and garnished with cheese, made a good start, and she even managed to eat a chunk of the crusty bread she had bought the day before. With two more cups of coffee to wash it all down, she felt distinctly stronger when she got up from the breakfast bar, and her optimism flowered as she washed her dishes and made her bed.

She was deep in contemplation of a cookery book she

had found on the shelf above the draining-board when the doorbell rang. Frowning, she glanced at her watch. It was just after ten o'clock. Too early for Ben, but not too early for Mrs Cipriani.

Sighing, she put the book to one side and went to answer the door. Although it was several years since she had spoken to Ben's housekeeper, that prospect didn't faze her. The little Italian woman had always been kind to her, and Cass had suspected that part of the reason had been Mrs Cipriani's antagonism towards Ben's mother. The two women had never got on, each resenting the other's influence in Ben's life. From Sophia's point of view, Mrs Cipriani was usurping the role which she thought properly should have been hers; while Mrs Cipriani regarded Signora Scorcese as an interfering harridan who couldn't quite accept that her son was not her responsibility any longer.

Fixing a polite smile on her face, Cass flung open the door, and then fell back aghast at the sight of the man who was standing just outside. 'Roger!' she whispered weakly, remembering too late that she should have checked first before being so impulsive. But it was too late now, and Roger Fielding took full advantage of the fact.

'I knew it!' he declared harshly, forcing his way past her and into the hall. 'I knew you'd be here. I just knew it! Your father was sure you'd gone to the States to stay with Marie Lee Piper, but my instincts were the right ones. You came running to dear brother Ben!'

Realising that with the door open his raised voice could probably be heard throughout the building, Cass felt obliged to close the door. So far as she remembered, there were two other tenants: one in the basement, and the other on the ground floor. Ben's apartment occupied the top floor of the old building and, although the walls were thick, the stairwells created an acoustic resonance.

'What do you want, Roger?' she asked now, leaning back against the cool panels, and his face contorted. He was a handsome man in the normal way, with stocky, well-bred features, and curly russet-brown hair. He was reasonably fit: he played tennis in the season, and squash when he could find the time. He even rode to hounds, whenever he was able, and Cass knew he was known as a very decent chap among his contemporaries. From her own point of view, the picture was somewhat different. Apart from his sexual proclivities, which she was inclined to blame herself for, he was disposed to be short-tempered, and mean with the staff at their London home. He couldn't penny-pinch with her, because her father gave her a very generous allowance, but, like many people who had not been brought up with a freedom from financial worries, he resented spending money on anyone but himself. Cass had sometimes wondered what kind of a life she would have had if her father had not been around to ease the burden, and it was frightening to think that one day Roger would be in control of the company.

Now he scowled. 'What kind of a question is that?' he snapped. 'What do you think I want? I want to know what the hell you think you're doing running out on me like that? Couldn't you at least have told me face to face what you planned to do? Instead of leaving notes and sneaking off, as if I didn't deserve an explanation.'

Cass sighed, and straightened away from the door. 'I think you'd better come into the living-room,' she said, passing him with a scarcely perceptible twist of her body to avoid brushing against him. 'Do you want some coffee? I think there's some in—'

'Damn you, I don't want anything! Except some answers,' said Roger angrily, obliged to follow her never-theless. 'Where the hell have you been hiding out? I've been to this apartment at least a dozen times already.'

'You have?' Cass could hear the tremor in her voice and struggled to control it.

'Yes.' Roger regarded her beneath lowered brows. 'Do you have any idea of the embarrassment you've caused me? It's been the devil's own job convincing your father that our marriage is not on the rocks.'

Cass swallowed. 'And isn't it?'

'No.' Roger glowered at her, and then, as if unable to sustain the grey directness of her gaze, he bent his head. 'Oh—I suppose this has something to do with my friend-ship with Valerie Jordan, doesn't it?' he muttered. 'Well, for heaven's sake, a man's entitled to some female com-panionship, isn't he? Goodness knows, I get little enough of it at home. It's nothing serious. She just makes me feel good, that's all.'

'Feel good?' echoed Cass bitterly. 'Is that what you call it?' Her lips twisted. 'And how much longer is this—friendship—likely to last this time? A week? A month? *Six* months?'

'I don't know.' Roger was resentful now, and he raised his head again, as if realising he was going to gain nothing by pleading with her. 'What does it matter? You can't pretend you're jealous. Why shouldn't I have a little fun if I want to? I've got little enough in my life as it is.'

Cass caught her breath. What was he saying? Could he possibly be offering her an escape, after all? Squaring her shoulders, she said quietly, 'I agree.'

'You agree?'

Roger was clearly taken aback at this, and Cass gained a momentary advantage. 'Yes,' she said with more con-fidence, 'I agree. We have nothing in common. I've thought so for—for a long time. And I'm quite prepared to give you a divorce.'

'*What?*' Roger's expression changed from disbelief to sudden fury. 'What the hell are you talking about? I said nothing about divorce.'

'But you said—'

'Damn you, I know what I said, and divorce did not figure in it at all. Do you think I'm crazy?' he stared at her as if she and not he had gone mad. 'Do you honestly think I'm going to walk out of this marriage, just because I've been a naughty boy?' He uttered a short, bitter laugh. 'You bitch! Did you really think that running away, embarrassing me in front of your old man, would make me consider giving you your freedom?'

Cass held up her head, her fragile hopes splintering beneath the onslaught of his savage words. 'You—you can't make me live with you,' she got out unsteadily. 'I'm not a child—'

'No. No, you're not a child,' conceded Roger, narrowing the space between them to stare at her with vengeful eyes. 'But you know what your father will say when he finds out what you're thinking. He wants this marriage to work. He's invested a lot of time and trouble in giving me the kind of corporate education necessary to follow in his footsteps, and how do you think he's going to feel if you tell him *you* want a divorce?'

'He'll understand if I tell him you're having an affair—'

'He didn't before.' Roger sneered. 'And what if I tell him about you? About how you feel about sex? How you've refused to sleep with me? The reasons why we haven't given him the grandson he's so desperate to have?'

'You wouldn't!'

'Wouldn't I?' Roger stepped nearer, and although she tried to get out of his way his hands fastened loosely about her throat. 'I would, believe me. I'd do whatever's necessary to prove it's not my fault this marriage isn't working. What would I have to lose? Self-respect doesn't mean much when you're fighting for your life!'

'Don't—don't be melodramatic!' Cass lifted her hands as she spoke to try and free herself from his grasp, but his grip was merciless. 'You—wouldn't be—fighting for your life. Only you could see it that way.'

'Well, whatever way I see it, that's the way it is,' retorted Roger imperviously, his expression mirroring his enjoyment at having her helpless in his hands. His fingers brushed the soft underside of her jaw. 'So why don't you go and pack your case, like a good girl, hmm?'

'No!'

Roger's hands tightened, almost threateningly. But he wouldn't kill her, she thought painfully. That would achieve the exact opposite of what he had come here for.

'Don't say that,' he told her after a hostile moment. And then, switching tactics again, his hands gentled to a lover's caress. 'Oh, Cass, *Cass*!' he breathed, lowering his mouth to brush the corner of her mouth with his lips. 'If you would only stop fighting me, we could have such a good time together. I'm not a possessive man. I don't need total fidelity. I wouldn't object if you had a little—fun, now and then. Just as I do—'

'Let go of me!'

With a superhuman effort Cass tore herself out of his arms, rubbing her bruised neck with frantic fingers, as if by this means she could erase his touch from her skin. She felt humiliated, abused; but most of all she was afraid of the power he had over her. She knew, without a shadow of a doubt, that what he had said about her father was true. So far as Guido was concerned, Roger was the son he had wanted Ben to be. She knew Ben had let him down. When it had come to the crunch, Ben had not been prepared to sacrifice his own ambitions for the company, and Cass knew how much that had hurt her father. So how could she let Roger tell Guido the truth about their marriage? That she had only married him on an impulse, that the physical side of their marriage was a farce, and that she had driven Roger to turn to other women? That they would never have the grandson her father wanted so long as they continued to occupy separate rooms?

Roger was rapidly losing what little patience he had. She could see it in his face, and it terrified her. And he held all the cards. He knew it and she knew it, just as she had known that this sojourn in Italy could only be a temporary escape. She was a coward, perhaps, but the idea of Roger telling her father the truth about their marriage had always deterred her. Guido wouldn't understand, never in a million years. It would ruin their association, and she couldn't bear the thought of losing the special relationship they shared. He was still old-fashioned enough to regard a woman's role in marriage as sacrosanct. Despite his divorce from Sophia, he still considered her his responsibility, and the alimony he paid was far in excess of any settlement given to her in a court of law. Even Diana was obliged to be obedient, for all her much-vaunted views on female emancipation, and Cass guessed there would have been brothers and sisters if her mother had not developed an infection after her birth which made any future pregnancies inadvisable. To hear that his daughter, the only child of his flesh, as he was wont to say in moments of extreme emotion, was deceiving him, would hurt him deeply, and although she wanted her freedom, some costs were just too high to pay.

'Well?' Roger demanded now. 'What are you waiting for? Go and collect your things. We're leaving.'

'No!'

In spite of everything, Cass hung back from that ultimate submission. Dear heaven, she thought, if she was to be forced to go home, at least she would have some time to herself first.

'What do you mean? No?'

Roger came towards her again, and she put out her hands to forestall him. 'I mean—no. I'm not coming with you. Not yet, at any rate,' she got out unsteadily. 'Ben—Ben's mother says I can stay with her for a while, and—and I'm going to.'

'Like hell you are!' Roger was incensed. 'You're coming back with me today, even if I have to drag you into the plane!'

'N-o!'

Cass's cry was protracted as he reached for her, his hand brushing her jaw painfully as she tried to turn away and he snatched at her shoulder. She felt his nails score her cheek and then his fingers managed to get purchase on a handful of the sloppy T-shirt, arresting her progress and jerking her back against him.

'Yes,' he contradicted her grimly, getting an arm about her waist. As his knuckles touched her breast, he uttered a hoarse oath. 'Bitch,' he muttered, taking hold of her breasts with callous fingers, and squeezing them cruelly. 'I'm going to teach you a lesson you won't forget, and you'll be too *pregnant* to make a fool of me again—'

'*Let her go!*'

The controlled yet implacable command caused Cass to let out a little shriek of relief. Although Roger made no immediate move to obey the words, his grip on her breasts was released, and Cass breathed a little more freely as the pain he had created subsided.

Swinging round, still holding her like a shield in front of him, Roger confronted the man who was standing in the open doorway with unconcealed dislike. 'Well, well,' he said, apparently undaunted. 'The prodigal returns. I wondered how long it would be before you put in an appearance. Well, may I remind you, Cass is my wife, and if you have any sense you'll stay out of my way.'

'I said, let her go,' repeated Ben levelly, but evidently Roger was unaware of the dangerous gleam in his eyes, Cass decided, torn between a desire to let Ben make her decisions for her, and a fear of what might happen if he did.

'—off!' retorted Roger, using a word that Cass had never before heard used in her presence. Abandoning his stance by the door, Ben purposefully crossed the room.

She thought then that Roger had realised his mistake and tried to rectify it, but it was too late. Although her husband pushed her violently towards the other man— maybe in a belated attempt to satisfy his demands, maybe to create a diversion, she wasn't sure—Ben simply put her gently aside before grasping Roger's shirt front and hauling him up in front of him. Then, thrusting his face close to the younger man's, he stared at him contemptuously for a moment, before saying in a low, almost pleasant, tone, 'If you ever lay a hand on her again, I'll kill you.'

'Get your hands off me!'

With hands that were not quite steady, Roger succeeded in freeing himself from Ben's grasp, but only, Cass suspected, because Ben allowed him to do so. There was no comparison between the two men: Roger might be fit and stocky, but he didn't have the height or the tensile strength of his adversary. While he had been at college, Ben had belonged to a martial arts group, and, although she doubted he still practised regularly, the discipline was still there in every line of his lean, muscular frame.

'I suggest you leave,' Ben invited now, giving Cass a brief appraisal, as if to reassure himself that she really was all right. His eyes narrowed when he saw the weal that Roger's nails had left along the side of her face, but he didn't mention it. He merely waited for her husband to obey his command.

Roger was sullen. 'Cass is coming with me.'

'No, she's not.'

Ben's tone was implacable, and Roger turned to his wife, his expression eloquent with meaning. 'Aren't you?'

Cass caught her breath. 'I—I—'

'I've told you. She's staying here,' inserted Ben flatly, as Cass struggled with her conscience. 'You can tell her father she's spending the next few weeks at Calvado. If he wants to get in touch with her, he can contact her there.'

Roger flexed his shoulders and checked his tie, a defiant gesture, Cass suspected, to prove to Ben he was not intimidated by his presence. Then, catching her eyes upon him, he held her gaze. 'And that's your decision, is it?' he enquired. 'You're sure you don't want to change your mind?'

It was a threat, pure and simple, and for a moment Cass was half persuaded to give in. But then, what it would mean to go back with him, to give up these few weeks of freedom, swept over her once again, and in spite of her fears she knew she couldn't do it. Not yet, at any rate.

'No,' she said now. 'No, I don't want to change my mind. Like I said earlier, I need—some time. We both do. And—and if you can't live with that—'

She broke off abruptly, realising she had said enough. It was up to Roger now. If he went to her father it would be all over, either way. And just at that moment she didn't much care what he did.

CHAPTER FIVE

THE DOOR slammed behind him, and it wasn't until its echoes died away that Cass realised she had been holding her breath. Then she took a shuddering gulp of air, and turned to look at Ben.

He hadn't moved. He was still standing on the spot where he had practically lifted Roger off his feet. He wasn't looking at her. His gaze seemed to be fixed on the distant spire of a church, visible through the open window, and if she hadn't known better she might have thought he was completely immune from the scene that had been enacted only minutes before.

Shivering a little, as much from reaction as from any feeling of chill, Cass pushed nervous hands through her hair. Then, gathering her composure, she walked across the room.

'I—I'm sorry you had to hear that,' she murmured, stopping in front of him and forcing him to look at her and not at the view. 'Um—I had no idea he would come here. He must have got the address from Daddy.'

Ben's eyes were still distant as he met her anxious gaze. 'And how long has he been here?' he enquired flatly.

'How long?' Cass blinked. 'Er—not long. Fifteen minutes, maybe.'

Ben's face was inscrutable. 'Fifteen minutes,' he echoed. 'Is that all?'

'Yes.' Cass licked her lips. 'Don't you believe me? I thought it was Mrs Cipriani. That's why I opened the door. If I'd known it was Roger—'

'You wouldn't have?'

'That's right.' Cass swallowed. And then, almost defensively, 'He—he's not usually like that, you know. I—I made him angry.'

Ben's nostrils thinned. 'But you didn't want to go with him. Did you?'

'No.' Cass shook her head. 'No, of course not.'

'Are you sure?'

'Yes.' She moved her shoulders a little jerkily. 'You must know that.'

'Must I?'

'Yes.' Cass didn't understand his attitude. Moments before, he had seemed so supportive. But, now that Roger had gone, she wondered if he was having second thoughts. 'You—you haven't changed your mind, have you? You don't think I should have—gone with him?'

Ben's mouth compressed. 'With that brute?' he demanded harshly, and Cass's knees went weak with relief. 'If I'd had my way, you would never have married him.'

But you don't know why I did, thought Cass bitterly, a little of her exhilaration fading at the memory. Still, at least Ben wasn't blaming her for what had happened. And thank goodness he had arrived back as he had. She had never seen Roger in such a temper, and without Ben's intervention she didn't know what he might have done.

'Then—then that's all right, isn't it?' she managed, a little tremulously, finding the courage to brush his bare arm with her fingers. He was wearing brown cord trousers and a beige cotton shirt, and he had rolled back the sleeves over his forearms. His skin was warm and brown, and rather liberally spread with fine dark hair, and her nails stirred the filaments, causing a disturbing feeling in the pit of her stomach.

Consequently, she jumped rather badly when his other

hand came to cover hers, compelling her palm against the heated flesh above his wrist. Her eyes lifted to his face then in some amazement, and she flinched when he asked her savagely, 'Why didn't you tell me you were pregnant?'

'Pregnant?' Cass gazed at him aghast. 'Wherever did you get that idea?'

'Where did I get it?' Ben uttered a sound of aggravation. 'Cass, Roger was taunting you about it when I came in!'

'Roger was?' Cass shook her head uncomprehendingly, and then suddenly her face cleared. 'Oh—*Roger*!' she exclaimed, as the memory came back to her. 'I know what you mean now. But that's not what he was saying.'

'No?' Ben didn't sound convinced.

'No.' Cass looked down at his hand imprisoning hers, and as if sensing her awareness Ben abruptly released her. 'No, it wasn't like that,' she added, wishing she had not drawn his attention to his grasp. 'I—well, I should say it was virtually impossible, as things stand.' She flushed. 'You see—it's been some time since Roger and I shared a bedroom, let alone a bed.'

'Are you serious?' Now it was Ben's turn to stare at her.

'Yes.' Cass lifted her head. 'I suppose you think that that's some justification for Roger's behaviour, hmm?'

'I didn't say that.'

'You didn't have to.' Cass took a deep breath. 'It's true. I'm not much good as a wife.' Her lips twisted. 'I'm not much good at anything.'

Ben frowned, evidently absorbing what she was saying. Then, 'Does—your father know this?'

Cass's head swung round. 'No,' she replied shortly. A

trace of resignation entered her voice. 'Are you going to tell him?'

'Me?' Ben shook his head a little grimly. 'Why should I want to do that?'

'I don't know.' Cass didn't know anything any more. 'I just thought—oh,' she spread a helpless hand, 'you might feel less sympathetic.'

Ben stared at her for a few moments longer and then turned away, raking back his hair with a restless hand. He was obviously disturbed by what she had told him and, although he had not said he was going to speak to their father, he had avoided a direct answer.

'I'll pack my things,' said Cass abruptly, making the decision for him, and he swung about to block her exit.

'No.'

'Yes.' She squared her slim shoulders. 'It's obvious how you feel. You thought I was the poor betrayed wife, and now you find out that's not exactly how it is, you're confused. Well, don't worry. I can handle this on my own—'

'Don't be stupid!' With an oath in his own language, Ben grasped the hands she was using to express herself, and imprisoned them between his own. 'There's no way I'm going to let you walk out of here. Pregnant or otherwise, you're staying with me—or at least, with my mother. Maybe in a few weeks you'll be able to see things more clearly. When you've had some time to rest and recuperate.' His fingers brushed the delicate bones of her wrist, which were almost visible through their thin veil of flesh. 'And put on some weight,' he added, a faintly humorous glint appearing in his dark eyes. 'I think that's one thing I can rely on Sophia to do.'

'Oh, Ben!' Cass caught her breath. 'I do love you.'

'And I love you,' he assured her crisply, but he released

her hands almost immediately, and she knew she had once again overstepped the bounds of their relationship. She would have to be careful not to do that too often, she reflected tensely, blinking back her tears. After all, it was one thing to ask for his help, and quite another to expect something more...

Despite the tensions that had greeted Ben's return, the rest of the day passed fairly smoothly. Cass prepared some lunch, which neither of them did full justice to, and in the afternoon she washed some clothes, checking over the things she had brought with her and which she intended to take to Calvado. She had packed mostly casual garments, in hopeful anticipation of staying at the villa, and anything else she needed she could buy in Porto Camagio, or Calvado itself.

Ben spent most of the afternoon at his desk, catching up on his mail, she thought, and doing a little work. She didn't particularly share his interest in medieval Italian history, but she did find the lives of the Medicis and the Borgias fascinating; and after she had put her own underwear, and several shirts of Ben's she had found stuffed in the clothes basket, into the dryer, she made a cup of coffee and brought it to him.

'Was she really as beautiful as they say?' she asked, leaning on the desk beside him, her hip against his arm, flicking through the pages of a book about Lucretia Borgia. She had found the biography while she was dusting the day before, and left it on top of the pile of books on the desk. 'Her brother evidently thought so. Isn't he supposed to have been in love with her himself?'

'I doubt if love ever entered into Cesare Borgia's scheme of things,' retorted Ben shortly, removing the book from her hands and tossing it across to the other side of the desk. He shifted a little pointedly, so that she was obliged to move away from him. 'Thanks for the coffee. When you're working, a drink is very welcome.'

But not company, finished Cass silently, acknowledging the rebuke. She forced a tight smile and left the room, but once she had gained the sanctuary of the bedroom her hard-won control deserted her. Sinking down on to the bed, she gave in to the tears that had been threatening ever since Roger had forced his way into the apartment, and it was several minutes before she regained her composure. But there was relief in the tears; relief, and a certain amount of resignation. No matter how sympathetic Ben might feel towards her, there were limits to his generosity. He saw her as his younger sister, nothing more, and the iniquitous attraction she felt towards him had to be squashed once and for all.

She had taken another shower and was sitting at the dressing-table, towelling her hair in the golden light of early evening, when there was a tentative knock at the bedroom door. 'Cass? Cass, can I come in?'

Cass hesitated, casting a dubious look at her reflection in the mirror. The apricot satin wrap, which was all she was wearing, was modest enough, but would Ben see it that way?

'Cass!' His voice was vaguely concerned now, and she realised her prevarication was creating exactly the wrong impression.

'Yes,' she answered at once this time, and then her eyes widened in surprise when the door behind her opened. Through the mirror, she saw Ben come into the room and then halt, somewhat impatiently she felt, when he became aware of her state of undress.

'Oh,' he said flatly. 'You're all right, I see.'

Cass turned on the stool, rubbing the ends of her hair

with the towel, for all the world as if her hands were not shaking. 'Shouldn't I be?' she countered, shrugging her slim shoulders.

'I thought I heard—well, obviously I was wrong,' said Ben, a little grimly. Then, half reluctantly, 'There's a hairdryer in the drawer beside you, if you'd prefer it.'

'Is there?'

Cass turned again to look doubtfully at the several drawers confronting her, and she heard him suppress some unspeakable comment before covering the space between them. He squatted down on his haunches to pull open the bottom drawer of the dressing-table, and then uttered another stream of Italian at the jumbled state of its contents. Obviously, someone had riffled through the drawer at some other time and left it in disorder. Men's socks and briefs in a variety of colours tumbled out on to the floor as he searched for the hairdryer, and Cass slipped off the stool to gather up the offending items. A pair of gold and white striped trunks with the word 'Tiger' insinuated across the crotch caught her attention, and she was gazing at them with a curious feeling of outrage when Ben snatched them out of her grasp.

'A joke,' he declared raspingly, having found the elusive dryer and pausing in the task of bundling all the underwear back into the drawer again. 'Here.' He handed the appliance to her and got to his feet. 'Let me know when you're finished. I'd like to take a shower myself.'

'Oh—well, I can dry my hair anywhere,' murmured Cass, scrambling up, too, and facing him with some embarrassment, but Ben merely shook his head.

'No sweat,' he replied coolly, walking back to the door. 'Take your time. I'm in no hurry.'

But after he had gone Cass found herself hurrying automatically. This was his bedroom, after all; his bathroom.

Just because he was kind enough to let her sleep in here, there was no reason for her to think she could monopolise the place all day as well as all night.

When she entered the living-room again, some minutes later, she was more suitably attired in lightweight cotton slacks and a toning silk vest. Her hair, dry now and silkily straight, hung loose against her shoulders, accentuating the delicate colour that a week in a hot climate had added to her skin.

'It's all yours,' she told Ben lightly, avoiding another possible rebuke by seating herself on the couch, the full width of the room between them. 'Um—what time would you like to eat? I've got some veal and some pasta—'

'I thought we might eat out tonight,' Ben interrupted, silencing her. 'As it doesn't much matter who sees you now, I suggest we have dinner at a small restaurant I know, just a few miles out of the city. It's not a particularly sophisticated place, but the food's excellent.'

'Oh, great.'

Cass swallowed her disappointment and tried to look enthusiastic. But she had been anticipating spending their last evening together alone at the apartment, and it was incredibly difficult to summon up any excitement about going out.

However, Ben seemed to notice nothing amiss, and went off to take his shower, unaware of her misgivings. But it did give her the problem of deciding what to wear, and while she washed up Ben's coffee-cup she mentally reviewed the limitations of her wardrobe.

Ben reappeared, sleek and overtly masculine, in close-fitting black trousers and a matching silk shirt. His dark hair, still wet from his shower, showed its length by brushing his collar, but Cass thought it suited him that way. She had always found him good to look at, but tonight he had a disturbing appeal that was purely sexual. It made her wonder if the inscribed underwear had been just a joke, or were there women in Ben's life of whom she was completely ignorant? It would be unusual if there were not, she acknowledged, brushing aside her own contention at the thought. Just because he worked at a scholarly occupation, it was no reason to imagine he lived like a monk. All the same, it made her realise how little she really knew about his private affairs, and it was disturbing to discover how possessive her feelings were.

Getting into the low-slung Porsche later that evening, she wondered if she had been altogether sensible in her own choice of attire. She had decided on a very feminine chiffon dress, tinted in shades of peach and apricot, whose flowing sleeves and layered skirt were very flattering to someone as slim as she was. But as she got into the car the skirt belled about her knees, exposing a generous length of her thigh and drawing attention to the shapely curve of her bare legs. She quickly tucked the folds of the dress about her, but not before Ben had observed her loss of dignity, and her cheeks were pink as he put the car into gear.

But at least it diverted her attention from the vehicle and the memories it held for her; though, as Ben wove his way in and out of the traffic, she couldn't help remembering the first time he had taken her out in it.

'All right?' Ben asked, indicating the open window beside him, and she nodded.

'Fine,' she confirmed, even though the breeze was tangling her hair into knots. Anything was better than sitting there with her face like a beetroot, she thought. And the breeze was very appealing after the heat of the day.

The Restorante Domenico was situated in a small village in the hills, a dozen or so miles from the city. Judging by the number of vehicles parked outside the well-lit entrance, its reputation was already well-established, and Cass ran hasty fingers through her hair as Ben locked the car.

An arched gateway ran through gardens already flood-lit, although it wasn't yet really dark. The scent of jasmine and bougainvillaea was intoxicating, and a small marble statue tumbled water into a stone basin.

Beyond the gardens, tables were set on an open-air patio, as well as inside in a beamed dining-room. Candles, burning inside glass globes on every linen tablecloth, illuminated the gleaming silver and delicate crystal. A four-piece band played unobtrusively in the background, and one or two couples were already using the tiny dance-floor, evidently content just to sway with the music.

'Scorcese,' said Ben to the white-aproned waiter who approached them, and received a beaming smile in return.

'In casa o all'esterno?' he requested, and Ben looked at Cass.

'Inside or out?'

'Oh—outside, please,' she exclaimed, unwilling to sacrifice a minute of the velvety-soft air by eating indoors, and the waiter smiled again.

'Una buona decisione, signora,' he applauded, and led the way to a table at the far side of the restaurant, overlooking the lush beauty of the garden.

'So, what would you like to drink?' Ben asked, after they were seated. His lips twisted. 'Not cognac, I hope.'

'No.' Cass pulled a face. 'Um—Campari and soda, I think.'

'OK.' Ben looked up at the waiter who was hovering. *'Due Campari e soda, per favore.'*

'Sì, signore.'

The waiter departed to get their drinks, and Cass

propped her elbows on the table, supporting her chin with her hands. 'Hmm,' she said, looking about her with some satisfaction. 'This is nice.'

Ben inclined his head. 'I thought you'd like it.'

'I do.' Cass lifted her shoulders appreciatively. 'I'm so glad you suggested it.'

'Are you?' Ben's expression was difficult to read in the shadowy light. 'I got the impression you weren't exactly enthusiastic about coming out.'

'Oh.' Cass was glad of the concealing darkness now. 'Well, I admit, I was looking forward to practising my culinary skills again. But—this is nicer.'

'Is it?'

He seemed determined to disconcert her, and she was glad when the waiter reappeared with their drinks and the menus. However, he said he would be back later to collect their order, and left them to enjoy their aperitif.

Hoping to allow the subject to drop, Cass sipped her Campari and soda and looked at the view. It was possible to see the lights of Florence from their elevated position, and she pretended to be absorbed in identifying the various domes and campaniles that towered above the city. It was all incredibly beautiful, and for a few moments she was really entranced by the spectacle.

'We should talk about tomorrow,' said Ben abruptly, destroying her tranquillity. 'If we leave early in the morning, I can get back home before nightfall.'

Cass's lips parted in dismay as she looked at him. 'You're not staying?'

Ben gave an impatient snort. 'You didn't expect I would be, did you?'

Cass licked her lips. 'Well—not weeks, perhaps. Not until the university closes anyway. But I did think you might spend a few days—'

'I can't.' Ben was adamant. 'I have—work to do here.'

'All right.' Cass managed to accept that. 'So when will you be finished?'

Ben sighed. 'I don't think you understand. I'm not talking about my work at the university. I—well, I'm writing a book about Ambroise Giotti, the sixteenth-century historian. I'm hoping to finish it during the summer vacation.'

Cass's disappointment was crippling. 'You mean—you won't be spending any time at Calvado?' she choked, unable to keep the tremor out of her voice, and Ben cast an impatient look skywards.

'I—didn't say that, exactly,' he muttered. 'Naturally, I'll come and see how you're getting on.'

'Oh, wonderful!'

She was bitter, and he expelled a weary breath. 'Cass, you're not making this any easier—'

'I'm sorry.'

'And I have done what you wanted.' He paused. 'I didn't realise I had any part in your wish to spend a few weeks at the villa.'

Cass looked down into her glass with a feeling of remorse. He was right, of course. When she had first decided to ask Sophia if she could stay at Calvado, her only intention had been to give herself some time away from Roger, to think and decide what she was going to do about her marriage. But since she had come here, her original motivations seemed to have been obscured.

'I'm sorry,' she said now, cradling the glass between her hands and lifting it to her lips. 'You're right, of course. I don't know what I was thinking of.'

'Are you sure?'

Ben stared at her somewhat suspiciously, and with an

effort she raised a smile. 'Of course. Now, what are we going to eat?'

It was a tremendous effort to swallow any of the delicious food Ben ordered. They had *antipasto*, minestrone, and spicy lamb cutlets served with a selection of vegetables and a side salad. Everything was cooked to perfection, and with the meal they had some of the local Chianti, which sparkled in her glass in the candlelight. She should have been delightfully content—but she wasn't.

After the meal, Ben asked her if she'd like to dance. 'I'm not much good at it,' he admitted, when she accepted his invitation. 'But as it's dark, no one will notice. Except you.' He grinned. 'You'll have to kick me if I step on your toes.'

Cass managed a light rejoinder, and then allowed him to lead the way on to the dance-floor. As well as being dark, it was also fairly well-populated, and as she turned to face Ben an unwary elbow behind her propelled her into his arms. She hit the solid wall of his lean frame with a force he had not expected, and in consequence his arms closed around her with rather more strength than he would normally have used. It brought her close against the hard length of his body, and with her face pressed against the opened V of his shirt she was assailed by the feel and the smell and the taste of his warm skin.

'Idiota,' muttered Ben against her hair, his lapse into his own language an indication of his own disconcertment, but Cass was too bemused by her own reactions to move away, even when she was able to. There was such a feeling of security in his arms, and she slid her arms around his waist, as many of the other dancers were doing, and began to move sinuously in time to the music.

'Cass!' Ben said her name deep in his throat, the sound a mingled expression of both protest and resignation, but he didn't push her away. Instead, he linked his hands in the small of her back and followed her lead, allowing the sensuous touch of the music to flow over both of them.

It was a tantalising experience. For the first time in her life Cass felt totally at peace, and although she knew it was crazy she was finding it increasingly difficult to hang on to her identity at that moment. It would have been so easy to tilt her head back and look into Ben's face, knowing that if she did so their lips would be only inches apart. She had the overwhelming feeling that just then Ben would be unable to resist her, and the idea of his mouth touching hers—as it had done on that other unforgettable occasion—was almost unbearably exciting.

But the memory of that other occasion brought her abruptly to her senses. What had happened that forbidden summer when she was eighteen had destroyed her relationship with Ben for years to come, and she had no intention of spoiling things again. Even if what had happened had been as much his fault as hers, she could not risk losing him now, and with a little gulp she pulled herself together.

It wasn't quite so easy to restore their earlier cordiality. A break in the music enabled her to draw back from his arms without creating any awkwardness, and when she suggested returning to their table Ben instantly agreed. But she suspected he was perfectly aware of how close she had come to doing something completely reckless, and there was a definite air of restraint between them when they drove back to the apartment later.

The apartment itself was distractingly intimate, and Cass reflected that Ben was probably right to insist she left the next morning. Whatever—or whoever—was responsible, she was absurdly vulnerable where he was concerned, and until she had her life in order it was better not to tempt fate.

It was strange, she thought, how with Ben she never felt that sense of withdrawal she felt with other men. Perhaps she was frigid, as Roger had accused her. Perhaps the feelings she had for Ben didn't cause her to freeze up, because they didn't threaten her sexually. And yet, when he had held her in his arms, she certainly hadn't felt sisterly towards him. She had wanted him to kiss her, and that was why she had to leave.

'Um—shall I make some coffee?' she asked, hovering in the doorway to the kitchen, but Ben shook his head.

'No, thanks.'

'Well, thank *you* for a lovely evening, then,' she murmured, half relieved not to have to prolong their goodnights. 'I did enjoy it. And—and as you said, the food was—marvellous!'

Ben propped his shoulder against the doorframe, successfully blocking her exit. 'Is that why you ate so little?' he suggested drily. 'Because it was so—marvellous?'

Cass sighed. 'I'm afraid I don't have a very big appetite at the moment.'

'That wasn't my impression two nights ago.' Ben regarded her steadily. 'As I recall it, you had two helpings of pasta.'

'Who's counting?' Cass shrugged her shoulders, and then lifted one hand to rub the chilled flesh of her upper arm. 'You know how it is: sometimes you're hungry, and sometimes you're not. That's the way it is.'

'Is it?'

'Oh, Ben, stop baiting me!' Her cry was tremulous, and he groaned.

'I don't seem able to,' he muttered, straightening away from the door and coming towards her. 'For heaven's sake, Cass, we both know what's wrong with you. Don't look at me like that! Do you think I don't have any feelings?'

Her eyes widened when he reached her, but when he put his hands on her hips and pulled her towards him she went into his arms without a protest. For the second time that evening, she felt the overwhelming security of his embrace, and she pressed herself against him, uncaring just then of the consequences.

All the same, a belated twinge of conscience forced her to make a perfunctory protest. 'You're going to hate me for this, aren't you?'

'Why should I?' Ben's hand at her nape continued to massage the tense muscles. 'It may be the only chance we have. Do you want to throw it away?'

Cass caught her breath. 'But—but should we?' she persisted faintly. Then, in a rush of guilt, 'You're my brother!'

'No, I'm not,' retorted Ben savagely, surveying her startled face with a grim, intent gaze. 'Haven't you realised that yet, you crazy little idiot?'

Cass shook her head. 'But—what—how—?'

'Not now,' he muttered, looking at her mouth with disturbing hunger. 'And if you don't want me to touch you, you'd better stop me. Because as God is my witness, I can't.'

Cass couldn't speak. The blood was pounding in her head and through her veins and, although she had a dozen questions she wanted to ask, the overpowering needs he was arousing inside her took total precedence, and her actions were purely involuntary.

'Ben,' she breathed, her hands, which moments before had been trapped against his chest, sliding up to his neck and tangling in the thick black hair that brushed his collar. 'Oh, Ben! Ben, kiss me.'

For a moment she thought he had changed his mind, and her senses almost screamed their frustration. But then, with a groan, he lowered his head, finding her lips with unerring accuracy, and crushing them against her teeth with a painful intensity.

Cass was trembling, but she couldn't help it. Her experience of men was practically non-existent—apart from Roger, that was—and he had never made her feel like this. She knew what she wanted to do, what her instincts told her to do; but at the back of her mind was the knowledge that Roger had drilled into her—that there was something lacking in her make-up, some awful deficiency in her emotional composition, that prevented her from enjoying a sexual relationship. And it was true. She had never cared for sex. Even that first time in Bermuda had been more in the nature of an act of defiance, a childish urge to recover her self-confidence after the ignominy of that scene at Calvado, than any real desire to go all the way. She had lost her virginity, but not her innocence, and nothing Roger had done since had altered that situation. That was why, when Ben lifted his head, she was overcome by her own inadequacy, and she wondered how she had ever had the nerve to behave so wantonly.

'What's wrong?' Ben demanded now, his thick lashes narrowing eyes that were already dark with passion. 'Did I hurt you?'

'Yes. I mean, no! That is—' Cass shook her head helplessly. 'I can't explain.'

'You don't want me to touch you?'

'Yes.' Cass closed her eyes to hide the desperation she was feeling. 'Yes, I do.'

'Then open your mouth,' said Ben thickly, stroking her lips with his tongue.

'What? Oh, I—are you sure?'

It was with some misgivings that she obeyed his request, but when his tongue plunged into her mouth her legs went weak. The impact of his kiss tore deep into her stomach, igniting every nerve in her body, and flooding her loins with warmth. Whenever Roger had tried to kiss her this way, she had felt only distaste and revulsion, but with Ben it was a shattering experience. It showed her a little of what had been lacking in her life for so long, and hinted at other desires she had thought were beyond her reach.

He kissed her many times, long, drugging kisses that left her limp and clinging to him, but always eager for more. His hands caressed her arms, sliding beneath the folds of chiffon, and caressing the skin that ached for his touch. He stroked her breasts, his thumbs finding the delicate nipples that swelled beneath his hands. And then he cupped her small buttocks and brought her fully against him. The unmistakable thrust of his own arousal didn't disgust her, as Roger's had done. It excited her. And the moist pulse between her legs throbbed with a life of its own.

'Oh, Ben,' she moaned, aroused now in a way she had never dreamed she could be. 'Ben, make love to me!'

Ben's hands abruptly stilled. 'I can't,' he muttered hoarsely, burying his face in the scented hollow of her shoulder. 'Don't ask me that, Cass, because I can't!'

Cass shook her head, her brain struggling to escape the soporific effects of passion. 'Why not?' she protested, grasping handfuls of his hair and forcing him to lift his head and look at her. 'Why not?' She blinked, trying to remember exactly what he had told her earlier. 'When—

when I asked you about—about our relationship, you said—'

'I lied!' Ben interrupted her harshly, gripping her shoulders now and propelling her away from him. 'It was contemptible, I know, and I'm sorry, but the devil makes his own rules.' His hands dropped to his sides, and Cass swayed a little unsteadily in front of him. 'I suppose you hate me now. Well, that makes a change, doesn't it?'

Cass stared at him unbelievingly, a sick little pain making itself felt in the pit of her stomach. It couldn't be true. What had just happened couldn't be wrong. It had felt so good, so *right*. For the first time in her life she had begun to understand how it could be between a man and a woman, and her senses utterly rejected what he was implying. And yet—and yet, it had felt good before, on the beach at Calvado, and all that had brought her was a lifetime of marriage to a man she didn't love, and who only wanted her for her father's money...

Cass was sick twice: once immediately after Ben had walked out of the kitchen, and the second time in the early hours of the following morning. On the second occasion, as she was shivering over the basin, she heard a knock at the bathroom door and Ben asking, somewhat anxiously, if she was all right, but she didn't answer him. Instead, she stumbled across the floor, a paper tissue pressed against her lips, and slipped the bolt into place. It ensured there was no way Ben could walk in and witness her humiliation, and the distinctive click as it slid into place was an audible indication of her intentions. All the same, she waited some time before coming out. She was half afraid he might be waiting for her in the bedroom.

She was up again at first light, throwing all the clothes she had unpacked into the suitcase, and checking she had left no incriminating evidence in the bathroom. Then, dressed in a coffee-coloured silk jumpsuit, she carried her case through to the living-room, and carefully lifted the receiver of the phone off its rest.

'What the hell do you think you're doing?'

The harsh question almost scared her out of her wits, and she dropped the phone. The dangling receiver butted the scarred wood of the desk, and before she could rescue it Ben crossed the room and lifted it grimly back on to the rest. He was dressed, too, in the dark shirt and trousers he had been wearing the night before, and she wondered for a moment if he had been to bed.

'I said, what the hell do you think you're doing?' he repeated, infinitely more intimidating now that he was only an arm's length away from her, and Cass had to steel herself to face him.

'I heard you,' she replied, unable to prevent the shiver of apprehension that feathered her skin. 'I—as a matter of fact, I was phoning for a cab. I imagine there will be cabs about at this time of the morning, won't there? I mean, people do have to catch early flights, don't they?'

'And why should you want a cab?' enquired Ben coldly. 'I've said I'll drive you to Calvado, and I will.'

'I'm not going to Calvado.'

The words came out in a rush, and she watched as his expression darkened ominously. 'Like hell you're not!'

'I'm not.' Cass gathered a little confidence from the relief of having said it. 'I—I'm going back to London.'

'No, you're not.'

'Yes, I am.' She swallowed convulsively. 'You can't stop me.'

'Can't I?' His smile held no trace of humour. 'I shouldn't be too sure of that if I were you.'

'What do you mean?'

'I mean, I have no intention of allowing you to make a fool of me—or my mother.'

'I've not made a fool of anyone!' Cass was tremulous. 'Except, perhaps, myself.'

'Nevertheless, you are not going back to London.'

'How are you going to stop me?' She gulped. 'Rape me?'

A spasm of some emotion she couldn't identify crossed his lean, dark face. 'Don't be so stupid!' he muttered, and when she reached for the phone again his hand came down, imprisoning her fingers against the receiver. 'If that had been my intention, don't you think I would have had a willing accomplice last night?' he grated savagely. 'Now, stop behaving like a schoolgirl, and accept your responsibilities!'

Cass was able to tug her hand away from the phone, but only because he let her, and a terrible sense of weariness seemed to be invading all her bones. 'You can't make me go to Calvado,' she repeated, twisting her hands together. 'Not—not unless you want me to tell your mother what happened. I will, you know. You can't silence me altogether. Not unless you decide to kill me, and throw my body into the Arno.'

Ben closed his eyes for a moment. 'Oh, Cass,' he groaned, turning away from her as he spoke, 'stop talking such drivel! What do you want me to say? I've said I'm sorry. I've said I've behaved abominably. It was *all* my fault. I take full responsibility.' He sighed. 'And if it's any consolation to you, I promise it won't happen again. But,' he turned back to look at her again, 'I want you to go to Calvado. It's what you need, and my mother is expecting you. How am I supposed to explain that you're not coming, when I had the devil's own job persuading her to invite you in the first place?'

Cass shook her head. 'I can't.'

'Why can't you?'

'Because—oh, because I can't. Not—not after what happened.'

'What did happen?' Ben's mouth twisted bitterly. 'I kissed you, and you kissed me back. Big deal!'

'It wasn't like that, and you know it.'

'I know you're making far too much out of it.' Ben breathed heavily. 'For heaven's sake, Cass, I'd had too much to drink and so had you! That's why you were sick. Because you ate too little, and drank too much.'

'No.' Cass wouldn't accept that, appalled that he had known what she was doing. 'I felt sick—sick to my stomach! You lied to me, Ben. I'll never forgive you for that.'

'I'm not asking for your forgiveness,' he retorted flatly. 'I just want you to forget what happened last night, and go to Calvado this morning as planned, and relax. That's what you came here for, isn't it? Or has the idea of going back to Roger lost its abhorrence?'

She knew it hadn't. Indeed, the idea of seeing Roger again filled her with alarm. Even now, even after what had happened, she couldn't face the thought of going home, and Ben could tell from her expression that she had not thought about the consequences.

'Well?' he prompted, gripping the sides of his neck with his hands, and flexing his shoulder muscles wearily. 'Can we come to some decision here?'

Cass held up her head. 'And if I still refuse to come to Calvado?'

Ben expelled his breath on a sigh. 'Don't make me say it.'

'Say what?'

'Cass!'

'No. Say what?' She insisted.

Ben stared at her. 'I could be just as destructive as Fielding, if I chose.'

Cass pressed her lips together to prevent them from quivering. 'You mean—you mean—you're threatening to tell Daddy about—about Roger and me?'

'If that's what it takes to bring you to your senses, yes.'

Cass caught her breath. 'You—you bastard!'

'Yes, well…' Ben turned away as he spoke, so that she had to strain her ears to hear his next words. 'That's what I am, aren't I? And you'd better believe it.'

It was barely eleven o'clock when they drove down the widening track to the Villa Andrea. The journey from Florence had been accomplished in record time, but Cass had been only superficially aware of the speeds the Porsche was achieving. Ben had had the windows open, and the breeze coming in off the ocean had torn her concentration to shreds. Even so, there had been a wonderful feeling of catharsis in the mindless ferment of the wind, and for a while at least she had been able to lose herself in a purely physical liberation.

However, with the tiled roof of the villa visible below them, Cass made a determined effort to recover her equilibrium. It would be foolish to think she could confront Ben's mother in a less than composed frame of mind. Sophia would see through any subterfuge at once, and she had always had the uncanny knack of knowing when something was wrong.

In consequence, Cass felt compelled to reveal her fears to Ben. Although they had scarcely exchanged two words since early that morning, she could not enter his mother's house without at least making an attempt to restore a semblance of civility between them.

'I think—I think we should try and put what has happened behind us,' she ventured tentatively, but the look Ben cast in her direction was not encouraging.

'Do you?'

'Yes.' Cass took a breath. 'As—as you've forced me to come here, I should have thought the least you could do is meet me half-way.'

Ben's hands tightened on the wheel. 'Might I remind you that that was what I suggested in the first place?'

'Yes—well—' Cass's tongue circled her lower lip. 'I—agree with you. We can't meet your mother now—not talking to one another.'

Ben lifted his shoulders. 'Aren't we talking to one another now?'

'You know what I mean.'

'Do I?'

'Yes.' Cass bent her head. 'You haven't said a word since we left the apartment.'

'Have you?'

'No.' Cass sighed. 'That's what I'm saying. I think—I think we should.'

Ben's lips twisted. 'It's a little late now, isn't it? We're here.' He drew the car into the shade of the lemon trees. *'Fait accompli.'*

Cass looked at him uneasily. 'You won't—you won't phone Daddy, will you?'

Ben's mouth hardened. 'Why should I?'

'I don't know.' Cass was confused. 'I just don't want…'

'Your secret's safe with me,' retorted Ben flatly. 'It always was. You should have known that.'

Cass's eyes widened. 'You mean—if I had refused to come here—'

'Short of kidnapping you, there was nothing I could do.'

Cass felt a ridiculous lump in her throat. 'Oh, Ben—'

'Don't!' he said sharply. 'Here comes *Mamma*! I hope you're ready.'

Sophia Scorcese looked just as formidable as ever and, even though she had made a tenuous peace with Ben, Cass still felt ill prepared to deal with her. Tall and imposing, her floral silk dress complimenting a figure that was still elegant, despite a certain thickening about the waist, Ben's mother had always intimidated her as a child, and although she was a woman now Cass still felt a lingering sense of inadequacy. But she had to squash feelings of that kind, and, giving Ben an unknowingly entreating look, she thrust open her door and got out.

'Good morning, *signora*,' she murmured as Sophia reached them, dredging up the schoolgirl Italian she had once used quite fluently. 'It's good to see you again.'

Sophia's lips moved in the semblance of a smile, but her gaze moved to her son, getting out of the car behind the girl. Then, speaking in English as if to emphasise the fact that she spoke Cass's language much better than Cass spoke hers, she said, 'I hope you had a good journey.'

'Uneventful,' replied Ben drily, and only Cass understood the irony of that remark.

'Well, you certainly made good time,' commented Sophia in return, and Cass wondered if she was as transparent as Ben's mother made her feel.

'You—er—you're looking very well, *signora*,' she ventured, eager to change the subject. 'And—and I'd like to say how much I—appreciate your inviting me.'

Sophia's lips twitched. 'Thank Benvenuto,' she advised her tersely. 'It was he who insisted I could do no other. *Bene*, shall we go inside?'

Cass looked back at Ben as his mother started towards the villa, and he lifted his shoulders in a resigned gesture.

'Give her time,' he murmured in a low voice as she came to help him get her belongings out of the back of the car. 'What did you expect? That she'd roll out the red carpet?'

'No, but—'

'Are you coming, Benvenuto?'

There was a definite edge to Sophia's voice now, and with a grimace Ben slammed the car door and locked it. 'No sweat,' he called, pocketing the keys, and Cass saw his mother wince at his deliberate use of the English slang.

CHAPTER SIX

BEN left four days later.

Even though Cass had expected him to stick to his original intention to leave almost immediately, he succumbed to his mother's invitation to spend at least one night at the villa.

'I see so little of you, Benvenuto,' she reminded him reproachfully, pre-empting his words of apology. 'Is one night in your mother's house so much for me to ask? Surely, now that Cassandra is here, you cannot intend to ignore us.'

Cass held her breath at this announcement, but no caustic comment was forthcoming. 'Of course not, Mother,' he replied without heat. 'Naturally, I'm hoping to spend some time with—both of you. But, at the moment, I have work to do.'

Sophia sighed. 'Your book, I suppose.'

'My book,' he agreed.

'But don't you earn enough money at the university?' she protested. 'Must you work every free moment you get?'

Ben shrugged. 'Perhaps I regard it as a pleasure,' he remarked mildly, evidently used to this argument. 'In any event, I've got quite a lot of catching up to do. I've been away for over two months, remember? Victor probably thinks I'm suffering from a severe case of jet lag. I've hardly been into my office since I got back.'

Sophia grumbled on a little longer, but it was obvious she was inordinately proud of her clever son. She always had been. Cass remembered thinking, when she was younger, that half the reason Sophia resented her staying at the villa was because she was jealous of the time Ben spent with her. At the time, she had dismissed the thought as being unworthy of her, but now she was not so sure. Particularly after what had happened last night, she reminded herself painfully. What was wrong with her? What was wrong with all of them? And why, even now, was she dreading him going away?

The suite of rooms that had been put at her disposal were disturbingly familiar. Maria Alvaro, Sophia's housekeeper, showed her where she was going to stay before they had lunch, and as she bustled about, throwing open windows and twitching curtains into place, the little Italian woman expressed her delight at seeing Signorina 'Sandra again.

'It has been too long, *signorina—no, signora,*' she exclaimed, opening Cass's case and expressing her dismay at the jumble of its contents. '*Dio mio, che confusione!* Did you pack this, *signora?*'

'I'm afraid so.' Cass was rueful. 'Um—just leave it. I'll deal with it later.'

'*Ma no!*' Maria shook her head, tutting at the dress Cass had worn the night before. 'I will come back later and unpack for you, *signora.* For now, you must refresh yourself for lunch. *Ciao!*'

Left to herself, Cass kicked off her shoes and padded barefoot across to the long windows. Maria had left them ajar, and on impulse Cass stepped out on to the balcony, catching her breath at the beauty of the view. It was another perfect day, and the waters of the bay were smooth and inviting. She would have liked nothing better than to change into her bikini and go down to the beach, but she knew that was impossible; for today, at least. She and

Sophia had still to discuss the reasons for her being here, and until that was out of the way she was unlikely to relax. On top of which, she had the beginnings of a headache, which in the circumstances she didn't think was so extraordinary. It had been a traumatic twenty-four hours.

Looking over the rail of the balcony, she discovered that Ben had come to stand on the terrace downstairs. He and Sophia were apparently sharing a pre-lunch aperitif and, realising that if she was seen they might think she was spying on them, she turned and went back inside.

The guest-suite consisted of a small sitting-room, a dressing-room and bathroom, and a generously proportioned bedroom, with an enormous iron-posted bed. At fourteen years of age, she remembered, it had seemed much more impressive than it did now. Of course, in those days she had still been at boarding-school, and when she was at home she had slept in the nursery-suite. Now, however, she had her own house in Knightsbridge, and the Villa Andrea no longer seemed so imposing.

The colour scheme had been changed, she noticed. When she was here before, there had been a predominance of pink and white, whereas now, delicate shades of cream and gold were reflected in the figured satin bedspread and the rich, flowing curtains. The jumpsuit she was wearing might have been designed with these rooms in mind, she reflected drily, and, keeping her thoughts in this inconsequential vein, she went to wash her hands.

Lunch was a distinctly stiff affair, despite her own— and Ben's—efforts to the contrary, and she was quite glad when, after the meal, Ben invited his mother for a stroll. It enabled Cass to escape to her room, and after taking a cooling shower she lay down on the bed.

However, in spite of her attempt to relax, by early evening the headache which she had been fighting off all day had become quite unbearable. When Maria came to return the clothes she had taken away to press, she was most perturbed to find the young *signora* in some distress, and Cass found it incredibly difficult to reassure her. Wearing only the flimsy briefs which she had put on after her shower, her slender frame looked absurdly fragile, and she mistook Maria's open-mouthed concern for something else.

'*Mamma mia!*' the Italian woman exclaimed, clasping her hands to her chest, and staring at the girl as if she couldn't believe her eyes. '*Che c'é?*'

'I've got a headache, that's all,' explained Cass tiredly, propping herself up on one elbow and looking down at her small breasts somewhat ruefully. 'I'm sorry if I'm embarrassing you, but it's so hot! I can't bear the covers over me. I seem to be burning up.'

'Is so?' Maria put down the clothes she was holding, and came rather tentatively over to the bed. Then, touching Cass's forehead with cautious hand, she uttered a cry. '*Dio mio! Tu sei calda!*'

'I know,' said Cass weakly, but Maria was already scurrying out of the room. 'Oh, *no!*' Cass groaned, sinking back against the pillows. Now Sophia was going to be involved. All she had was a headache, for heaven's sake! Hadn't Maria the sense to understand that?

But when Sophia appeared she was not alone. Ben followed his mother into the room and, ignoring her horrified exclamation when she saw Cass's semi-nude body, he brushed past her and came to the bed.

'Cass!' he muttered, dropping down on to the bed beside her and covering her temples with his hands. 'You're on fire!'

'It's just a headache,' she whispered wearily, shifting

restlessly beneath his hands, and as she did so Sophia's
fingers grasped Ben's arm.

'This is not the place for you, Benvenuto!' she snapped
angrily. 'Come, let me see what is wrong. If the girl is
sick, she needs the *dottore*, not you.'

'I'm not ill,' persisted Cass, half tearfully. 'Ben, all I
need is a couple of aspirin. I'll be all right in the morning.'

'Will you?' The compassion in his dark eyes was almost her undoing, and she had to restrain herself from
throwing herself into his arms.

'Yes.'

'Benvenuto, this is intolerable! Will you get out of here,
or must I call Carlo and ask him to eject you?'

The idea of the elderly little Italian gardener being able
to eject a man of Ben's size and strength was ludicrous,
but her words had the desired sobering effect.

'I'll call Lorenzo,' declared Ben, getting to his feet with
some reluctance, and the tears Cass had been suppressing
would no longer be denied.

'I—I don't need a doctor,' she insisted, but Ben only
shook his head.

'I think perhaps you do, *cara*,' he disagreed ruefully,
and, dragging his gaze from hers he went out of the room.

In actual fact, Cass didn't remember much of the next
forty-eight hours. The doctor who arrived with amazing
promptness assured her that she was not wasting his time.
On the contrary, in his opinion she had caught a chill, and
in spite of her protests she was wrapped in an old flan-
nelette nightgown of Maria's, and covered with several
layers of blankets.

She didn't know much about the medication she was
given; all she remembered was the pain in her head, which
moved to her chest, and the blessed relief that came from

losing consciousness. She hadn't the strength to keep her eyes open, even when she was conscious, and images of Ben, Sophia, Maria and the doctor moved in and out of her vision, without her really knowing if they were real or imagined. She knew someone was looking after her, caring for her bodily functions and changing the bedlinen when it became drenched with the perspiration that poured out of her, but she was too weak to thank them. Day and night fused together in a mindless blend of misery, and there were times when she wished they would just leave her alone and let her die.

But she didn't die. Slowly but surely her body's immune system exerted itself, and presently, when Maria came to spoon chicken broth into her mouth, she didn't find it totally nauseating. On the contrary, by the end of the third day of her illness, she was actually able to hold the cup herself, and swallow the creamy broth with real enjoyment. She was even able to appreciate the sunset that was streaking the sky beyond her windows with vivid shades of red and amber, and acknowledge that in spite of everything she was glad to be alive.

Sophia appeared as Maria was tidying the bed, and Cass curled one fist inside the other as Ben's mother approached her. She wasn't sure that she was up to dealing with her old adversary yet, but she forced a tight smile to her lips and offered a tentative word of gratitude. After all, this was Sophia's house, and she was only a visitor here. It would have been quite reasonable for Sophia to insist she be taken to hospital to be treated; but she hadn't, and Cass was grateful.

'*Prego,*' declared the older woman indifferently. 'I am glad to see you are feeling better.' She waited until Maria had left the room, and then pulled a chair to the side of the bed. 'Can I get you anything?'

Cass shook her head. 'No. No, thank you. I'm fine.' She indicated the thin blanket which was all she needed now. 'I feel much cooler.'

'But not cold?' suggested Sophia swiftly, and Cass shook her head again.

'Just—comfortable,' she conceded. 'Thank goodness! That was some chill.'

'It was—how do you say it? *Polmonite.*'

'*Polmonite?*'

Cass didn't understand, and she jumped violently when a disturbingly familiar voice said softly, 'Pneumonia. You've had a mild form of pneumonia. It's lucky you were here, and not at the Villa Regina!'

'Benvenuto! What are you doing here?'

The impatience in his mother's voice was unmistakable, but Ben was not perturbed. 'The same as you, I expect, *Mamma,*' he replied evenly, coming to stand behind her chair. 'To see Cass—and to tell her about her father. You did intend to tell her Guido had phoned, didn't you?' He smiled at the angry look she turned in his direction. 'I thought so.'

Cass frowned a little anxiously. 'Daddy phoned?' she exclaimed. 'When?'

'Yesterday,' said Ben, before his mother could answer. His eyes on Cass were disturbingly gentle. 'How do you feel?'

'She is feeling much better,' declared Sophia tersely. 'And you know how I feel about you being in your sister's bedroom, Benvenuto. I wish you would go!'

Ben's eyes darkened as he looked at her, and his mouth lost its sensuous curve. 'Yes, I know how *you* feel, Mother,' he agreed tautly. 'But as Cass is obviously still very weak, I wanted to make sure you didn't upset her.'

'Benvenuto!'

Ben shrugged, unrepentant. 'Well, it's true.' He transferred his gaze to Cass's pale face. 'Your father just
wanted to make sure you were all right.'

Cass swallowed. 'You told him I was ill?'

'No.' Sophia cast her son another furious look. 'Apparently, Roger—'

'Not now, Mother.'

Ben's hand on his mother's shoulder had the desired
effect, and she pursed her lips irritably, but Cass wanted
to know what she had been going to say.

'Roger?' she said unsteadily, looking up at Ben. 'What
about Roger?'

Ben's fingers must have bit into his mother's shoulders
before he removed them, because she winced. But he
couldn't take back her words, and he knew it.

'Roger's told your father where you are,' he informed
Cass reluctantly. 'That's all. Just where you are.'

Cass struggled up on her pillows. 'And—and what did
Daddy say?'

Ben groaned. 'Nothing of importance,' he assured her
firmly, coming round his mother's chair and squatting
down beside the bed. He took one of her nervous hands
between both of his and smiled encouragingly at her.
'Honestly. He just wanted to assure himself that you really
were here.'

Cass quivered, the warmth of his fingers disturbingly
intimate in spite of his mother's presence. 'And—and did
you tell him I was ill?'

'We had to,' cut in Sophia curtly, getting to her feet
and forcing Ben to do the same. 'He is your father, *in fin
dei conti*.'

'Yes.' Compelled by Sophia's reproving gaze, Cass
drew her hand away from Ben's, and tucked it under the
covers again. 'Yes, of course. Was he angry?'

'Angry?' Ben made a sound of impatience. 'No, of course he wasn't angry. He was concerned. He—well,' he looked narrowly at his mother, 'he wants to come and see you.'

'No!' Cass knew she didn't have the strength to cope with her father at the moment. She had no doubt that both he and her mother were concerned about her, but she also knew that he would not be able to come here without bringing up the subject of her separation from Roger, and that was something she couldn't face right now.

'But, Cassandra—' began Sophia protestingly, only to have her words interrupted once again by her son.

'That's what I thought you'd say,' Ben declared flatly. 'And that's what I told him. I said you'd get in touch with him as soon as you were on your feet again. By telephone.'

Cass sighed weakly. 'Oh, thank goodness!'

'I just hope Guido understands that I had no part in this—this *sotterfugio*!' Sophia muttered. Then, after another warning glance from her son, she shrugged. '*Bene*, you are old enough to know what you are doing, I suppose. And who am I to plead Guido's cause? Has he ever pleaded mine?'

Cass caught her lower lip between her teeth, wishing Sophia would go so that she could talk to Ben alone, but that was clearly not to be.

'I think we should let Cassandra rest now,' the older woman suggested pointedly, taking her son's arm and guiding him towards the door. 'She has had quite enough excitement for the moment, and don't forget, you have to leave very early in the morning.'

'You're leaving?' Cass couldn't keep the note of desperation out of her voice as she endeavoured to raise herself on her elbows, and Ben heaved a sigh.

'I have to,' he said quietly. 'I've already spent much longer here than I had intended, and Victor's leaving for the States on Monday. I want to see him before he goes, and there's not a lot of time.'

'I see.' Cass slumped back against the pillows. She wanted to ask him when—*if*—he was coming back, but with Sophia logging their every move she didn't have the nerve. 'Well, take care.'

'I will.' Ben released himself from his mother's grasp, but he didn't come back to the bed. 'You, too. Don't overdo things. The doctor says it will be several weeks before you recover your strength.'

Cass nodded, pressing her lips together to prevent his mother from seeing how upset she was, and with a reassuring smile Ben followed Sophia out of the room.

Cass heard the Porsche leave the following morning. The sound of its powerful engine was unmistakable, and as she had been lying awake for most of the night it was not surprising that she heard the car accelerating up the track to the main road. It was then that the tears came, and she was glad there was no one around to witness her foolish collapse.

All the same, she had thought that he might come and see her once again before he left. Talking to him in his mother's presence had not been a very satisfactory arrangement, and, although she knew there was really nothing more to say, she was desperate enough to hope.

But he had gone without even saying goodbye, and she had no idea when she was likely to see him again. He might ring, of course, but as his mother was sure to answer the phone that too was an unsatisfactory proposition. Sophia was unlikely to encourage their friendship, in the present situation. She hadn't said anything yet, but Cass knew her views on the sanctity of marriage, and she was unlikely to be sympathetic.

It was a depressing situation, and she half wished she was still sick enough to require constant medication. At least in that trance-like state between the conscious and subconscious worlds she had felt no pain.

CHAPTER SEVEN

THREE weeks later, Cass rolled over on to her stomach to expose her back to the delicious warmth of the sun. The cove below the villa was the perfect suntrap, and as it was only accessible from the cliffs above it was invariably deserted. The occupants of the neighbouring villas were, for the most part, like Sophia Scorcese, middle-aged to elderly residents, to whom the climb both up as well as down the cliffs was irksome. In consequence, Cass often sunbathed completely nude, and her slim body had acquired an all-over, honey-gold tan.

She was feeling so much better, too. Three weeks of Sophia's cooking had wrought a definite improvement and, although her appetite was by no means large, she was eating, which was itself a transformation. Already the pepper and salt hollows had disappeared from her throat, and her whole body was acquiring a healthy coating of flesh. She wished Ben could see her, she was sure he would notice the difference; but since he'd left Calvado twenty-two days ago, she had heard nothing from him.

At first it had been hard to reconcile herself to his absence, and she knew Sophia had kept a close eye on her, as if she suspected Cass might find some way to communicate with Ben behind her back. But gradually Sophia had had to accept that coming here had been her decision, not Ben's, and the sooner she realised she was on her own now, the better.

But it was hard, and even now every nerve in her body quivered every time a car came down the wooded track.

Not that any of the cars ever stopped at the Villa Andrea—except the old Fiat belonging to Dr Lorenzo, that was. The doctor had come every day at first, but now he limited his visits to twice weekly. Although, Cass suspected, he had enjoyed coming more frequently, if only to sample Sophia's home-made ice-cream.

Her father had phoned several times, without waiting for her to phone him. But in the beginning Sophia had been surprisingly understanding, and made no bones about telling him that Cass wasn't well enough to come to the phone. 'She will phone you when she is stronger,' she had informed him stiffly, and Guido had had to be content with that.

When Cass did get to speak to him, however, he was remarkably sympathetic. He had been worried about her, that was obvious, and it had evidently hurt him that she should have chosen Ben to confide in and not himself.

'We could have worked something out, *cara*,' he exclaimed, after assuring himself that her health was no longer in jeopardy. 'Poor Roger, he is *distrait*! He misses you terribly.'

'Does he?' Cass was tempted to tell her father exactly how much Roger was missing her, but now was not the time to get into personal matters of that sort.

'But of course,' Guido insisted now. 'He loves you, *cara*. Oh, I know that sometimes he acts a little foolishly, but his heart is in the right place, no?'

'If you say so.'

Cass was non-committal, and she heard her father heave a sigh. 'Very well,' he said evenly. 'Perhaps you do need a little time away from one another. Absence makes the heart grow fonder, is that not what your mother says? Have your holiday, *figlia*. Enjoy yourself. And when you are ready, we will talk again.'

'Yes, Daddy.'

Cass was so relieved to escape so easily that his next words didn't immediately register, and he had to repeat them for her.

'You can tell Ben I shall expect a full explanation from him, also,' Guido declared smoothly. 'I am not at all convinced that this was all your own idea. Just remind him of his responsibilities, will you?'

'But, Daddy—'

But her father had rung off, and Cass replaced her receiver with a wry expression. Trust Guido Scorcese to have the last word, she thought somewhat mutinously. And, as usual, he had found someone else to blame.

It was the day after this conversation with her father that Ben's mother brought up the subject Cass had been trying to avoid. Since her illness and subsequent convalescence, she had hoped Sophia had decided to boycott the question of her marriage, but she should have known better. Evidently the Italian woman had only been biding her time until Cass was completely well again, and she apparently thought that if she was well enough to speak to her father, she was well enough to speak to her. Consequently, in the middle of supper that evening, she asked the girl outright what she intended to do when she left Calvado.

'I'm not sure.' Cass was not prepared for this, and her brain felt as organised as a sponge. 'I—need time.'

'How much time?' Sophia was not sympathetic now. She was distinctly unsympathetic, and Cass wished Ben was there to act as mediator.

But then she realised that this was exactly the kind of situation she was going to have to deal with from now on. If she ever hoped to make a life for herself, she was going to have to find the strength to defend her own decisions. Ben was not going to be around to help her. She had to accept that. And if she intended to stand up to her father, surely she could stand up to Sophia.

'I don't know,' she said now, determinedly helping herself to more of the delicious peppered kidneys that Sophia had made into a tasty *ragôut*. 'A few weeks, maybe.'

Sophia's lips compressed. 'Then you have not yet decided on divorce?'

Cass hesitated. 'No.'

'Good.' Sophia's expression softened a little. 'Marriage is not something that should be taken lightly. I know.'

Cass inclined her head, unwilling to get involved in any discussion of her parents' marriage, and after a few moments Sophia spoke again. 'But you realise that by coming here you have jeopardised Benvenuto's relationship with his father, do you not?' she exclaimed. 'It is obvious that Guido will blame Benvenuto for encouraging you in this. And bringing you here!' She snorted. 'He already blames me for Benvenuto's decision to refuse his inheritance.'

Cass refused to be daunted. She had been expecting this, for heaven's sake, she told herself. But she was disturbed to hear that apparently Sophia had not been behind Ben's decision to abandon his father's plans for him. Both she and her mother had assumed that Sophia had practised some form of emotional blackmail on him.

'I think Ben's old enough to handle Daddy, don't you?' she replied now. 'In any case, I shall tell him it was my decision. It was. And I'll deal with the consequences.'

'And your husband?' suggested Sophia bleakly. 'How will you deal with him? What explanation do you intend to offer for walking out on Roger?'

Cass sighed. 'I don't have to offer him any explanation. He knows why I walked out.' She paused. 'So does Ben.'

Sophia's nostrils thinned. 'I see.'

'Oh—' Cass could practically read her thoughts. 'There was another woman involved,' she told her wearily. 'Does that make things clearer? Roger is having an affair.'

'So?' Sophia held up her head, and Cass stared at her uncomprehendingly. 'Your father had many such affairs before Diana Palmer-Harris came along and demanded he abandon his honour and his integrity. Oh—did you think your mother was the first?' Sophia's lips twisted. 'Oh, no. She was just the cleverest, that is all.'

Cass caught her breath. 'That's—not true!'

'It is true.' Sophia regarded her pityingly. 'And if you expect any sympathy from that quarter, perhaps you should think again.'

Cass shivered. 'How do you know this? You were living in Genoa.'

'Do you think only English women find a powerful man like Guido Scorcese attractive?'

Cass shook her head. 'I've never thought of it.'

'No—well, why should you?' Sophia was unexpectedly understanding. 'You were not even born when this was going on.'

'No.'

Cass stared out across the terrace with unseeing eyes. Below the cliffs, the dark waters of the Bay of Porto Camagio lapped the cove, and overhead a pale moon cast its illumination on the night-scented vine that clung to the walls of the villa; but Cass was unaware of the beauty around her. She had never considered that her father might have had other women besides Sophia and her mother. Such a thought would have been abhorrent to her. But then, she had always regarded him as being totally above reproach. The idea that there could even have been women since Diana was a startling revelation. Was that why he had been so tolerant of Roger's infidelity? Because he saw him as a man after his own heart?

'Do not look so troubled, Cassandra.' Sophia's hand on her arm was surprisingly comforting. 'Maybe I should not have told you. After all, there can be no doubt that Guido loves you. And that is all that matters, *no*?'

Cass blinked, and endeavoured to recover her composure. 'I'm glad you told me,' she declared after a moment. 'In a way, it helps.' She paused, and then added curiously, 'So why didn't you try to stop Ben from associating with—with us? I mean, it must have been hard for you to—to accept that—that we were friends.'

Sophia's expression changed. Evidently their brief spell of conciliation was over. 'Benvenuto is Guido's son,' she stated coldly. 'I have never tried to come between them. It was Benvenuto's decision to choose a *professione scolastica*, not mine.'

Cass nodded. 'If you say so.' And, curiously enough, she did believe her. Although he loved his mother, Ben was nobody's pawn. Not even Sophia's.

That conversation had taken place over a week ago now, and since then things had been a little easier between the two women. Perhaps Sophia had realised that Cass, no more than herself, could dictate Ben's actions. Whatever, the Italian woman had made no further reference to Cass's leaving, and the sun and her surroundings were helping to heal her physically, at least.

The sun was hot, and Cass wriggled on to her side to consult her wristwatch, which she had left lying on the towel beside her. It was almost noon, time she was gathering her belongings together, and making the arduous climb up the cliff path. But she could have one last swim first, if only to allow the salt water to rid her flesh of its glistening coating of protective oil.

Wearing only her skimpy bikini briefs, she plunged into the clear water, catching her breath at its sudden chill. Although the temperature of the water was fairly warm, it always felt cold on first immersion, and she swam out eagerly from the shore to revitalise her limbs. She could swim quite strongly now. When she'd first come down to the cove, she had hardly dared go out of her depth, but now she had no such apprehensions. Every day she had worked herself a little harder, gradually building up her strength, and now she had the confidence to trust her own abilities.

It was when she turned back towards the beach that she saw the figure standing on the sand. With the sun in her eyes, it was difficult to see who it was, but it was definitely a man, and her spirits sank. The distance between the shoreline and the striped canvas bag that contained her clothes was several yards and, although she knew that topless bathing was quite common all along the coast, she had never exposed her breasts in public. Thank goodness she was wearing the briefs, she thought drily, remembering how a couple of times she had swum completely nude. In those circumstances, she would have had to remain in the water until whoever it was got tired of watching her. A chilly prospect, she reflected uneasily, recalling Dr Lorenzo's warning about not taking any unnecessary risks with her health. She would definitely be more circumspect in future.

Deciding she had little alternative but to face the consequences of her actions, she swam slowly back to the shore. And, determined to ignore whoever it was, who had no more discrimination than to stand and watch her, she splashed into the shallows. But, as she straightened to walk through the waves to the beach, her anxieties gave way to a disbelieving excitement. It wasn't a stranger on the beach, it was Ben. Abandoning any modicum of dignity, she practically ran out of the water into his arms.

'You're back!' she exclaimed incoherently, hugging him exuberantly, not immediately aware that he was not returning her embrace. 'Oh, why didn't you let us know you were coming? You could have rung! You are a selfish pig—'

She broke off abruptly when painful hands on her arms propelled her away from him. Then the towel she had been lying on earlier was thrust into her hands, and Ben said harshly, 'Cover yourself!'

Cass's enthusiasm for his return took a decided blow, but she took the towel obediently, and wrapped it sarongwise about her. Then, sustaining her smile with difficulty, she pulled a rueful face. 'Sorry,' she murmured, squeezing the excess of moisture out of her hair. 'I was just so pleased to see you.' She sighed. 'Do you have to be such a prude?'

'I'm not a prude!' If she had thought he was angry before, he looked positively furious now. 'I'd just like to know what you would have done if I'd been someone you didn't know!'

'Well, I wouldn't have thrown myself into his arms, if that's what you're afraid of,' remarked Cass, somewhat facetiously, but Ben was not amused.

'And what if they had *wanted* you to?' he suggested grimly. 'Or something not quite so civilised?'

Cass's shoulders sagged. 'Rape, you mean?'

'Or worse.' Ben stared at her malevolently. 'Does my mother know you bathe in the nude? Or haven't you dared to tell her?'

Cass flushed. 'I'm not in the nude.'

'No?' Ben was not convinced. 'That—that bikini leaves little to the imagination.'

'Well, everyone wears them,' retorted Cass indignantly. 'You've only to go to Alassio or Sestri—'

'Where there are crowds of people, female as well as male, for protection,' inserted Ben coldly. 'I thought you had more sense! If you have to swim, get yourself something decent to wear. A proper swimsuit would be an improvement. But best of all, don't swim alone.'

Cass gave him a sulky look. 'And don't sunbathe either, I suppose.'

'Not down here, on your own, no. The sun's just as hot on the terrace.'

'But I couldn't go in for a dip any time I felt like it, could I?' she argued.

'No.' Ben conceded the point. 'But you could always take a shower. And the public beach in Calvado is not that far away.'

Cass sniffed. 'Thank you.'

'Don't mention it.'

Ben thrust his hands into the pockets of the grey cotton trousers he was wearing and turned his attention to the sails of a yacht on the horizon, and Cass knew an overwhelming feeling of humiliation. For weeks she had been waiting for some word from Ben, anything to prove he had not forgotten all about her, now that she was out of his sight. But now, when he was here and she had shown how overjoyed she was to see him, he was behaving like a boor and a bully, and she hated him for making her feel like a fool, and she wished that she was dead.

The trouble was, she knew that he was right. It had crossed her mind before how lonely the cove was, and how inaccessible should she need to shout for assistance. But coming here, spending this time alone, had been all part and parcel of her need to prove her independence to herself, and now he had spoiled it, made her feel totally inadequate.

Snatching up her sandals, and the bag that contained her wrap-around skirt and cotton vest, she left Ben to his observations and strode away across the sand. With tears pricking at the backs of her eyes, she was in no state to conduct a conversation with him, or anyone else, and she started up the cliff path with blind determination.

'Hey!' Ben had evidently just realised what she was doing, and was following. 'Hey, Cass!' he yelled impatiently, coming up the steep path after her. 'Slow down, for heaven's sake. You'll give yourself a heart attack in this heat!'

'Well, at least then you won't have to bother about me any more,' she threw over her shoulder, not really caring if he could hear her or not. 'Go and watch the boats. I'm going to take a shower.'

'Don't be such a bloody little idiot!' he snarled, right behind her, and she almost over-balanced at the shock of finding him so close.

He was sweating freely, she saw, just as she was, and although he had loosened his shirt and pulled it out of the waistband of his trousers it was still plastered to his skin in places. Rivulets of moisture were trickling down his chest, drawing her attention to the growth of fine, dark hair that started just below his ribcage, and arrowed down beneath his belt. His hair was damp with perspiration, and he was breathing heavily, but it was the musky scent of his body that set every nerve in her body on edge.

'Go back,' she got out faintly, dragging her gaze away from him with some effort. 'I don't need any assistance. I've climbed this path a dozen times. And if it's any consolation to you, I shan't be coming down here again. You've made your point. As usual, I've been a fool!'

'*Cass.*' His use of her name was weary now, and when she summoned the nerve to look back at him she saw the tension in his face. 'Surely you know I was only thinking of you. I don't want you to get hurt. When I saw you down there, I really lost my head. If anything happened to you, I'd never forgive myself.'

Cass swallowed, and although she was absurdly tempted to lean back against the hard strength of his chest she forced herself to go on, rather less recklessly this time. 'It—wouldn't have been your fault,' she assured him, as they neared the top of the cliff. 'I'm old enough to know what I'm doing.'

'I brought you here,' he insisted.

'Because I asked you to.'

'But I've deliberately stayed away,' he retorted flatly, and when she came to an abrupt halt, he couldn't prevent himself from walking into her.

'Why?' she asked, as his arms closed automatically about her. 'Why did you stay away?'

'Don't be naïve,' Ben advised her roughly, pushing her determinedly up the last few feet of the path, until they were both on level ground again and he could release her. 'We both know the reasons.' His lips twisted. 'And now I think I need a shower, too.'

Cass hesitated. 'Are you staying?'

Ben took a deep breath and nodded. 'For a little while,' he conceded.

'How little?'

'That depends.' Ben pushed his hands into his trouser pockets again and began to walk towards the villa.

'Depends on what?' Cass persisted, hurrying to catch up with him, and he grimaced.

'Perhaps you should say, *on whom*?' he remarked drily. 'Which reminds me, I didn't ask you how you were feeling? Or is that an unnecessary question in the circumstances?'

Cass looked sideways at him. 'What circumstances?' she probed, and he regarded her with tolerant eyes.

'Do you want me to say it? OK. You look much better. Beautiful! Or should I say *bella*, like a good Italian?'

Cass smiled. 'Beautiful will do.' She glanced down at her towel-draped figure. 'How can you tell?'

Ben's mouth compressed. 'I saw, remember?'

'Oh, yes.' She knew he could tell from her expression that she hadn't forgotten at all. 'So you approve.'

'I think we've taken this far enough,' Ben retorted tightly. 'Have you spoken to your father?'

Cass gave him a resigned look. 'Yes.'

'And what did he say?'

'Not a lot.' Cass pulled a face. 'He just thinks I'm suffering some kind of mental aberration. He thinks I'll get over it.'

'I see.' Ben inclined his head. 'And what do you think?'

Cass lifted her shoulders. 'Am I allowed to have an opinion?'

'Don't be silly!'

'Well—' She was feeling emotional again, and now was probably not the time to be having a conversation of this sort. 'According to your mother, Daddy is hardly likely to consider Roger's little playmate a good enough reason for me to want a divorce. Apparently, he used to do much the same thing. Certainly before he married Mummy, anyway. Who knows what he's done since?'

Ben halted now, his expression mirroring his feelings. 'Sophia has no right to discuss Guido's affairs with you,' he declared irritably.

'Affairs being the operative word,' remarked Cass cynically.

'Don't be facetious!'

'I'm not.' Cass felt ridiculously near to tears. She took a moment to calm herself, and then said, 'Did you know what he was like? Did you know he had had mistresses? Are you like that, too? I'd like to know.'

Ben pulled his hands out of his pockets, and for a heart-stopping moment she thought he was going to strike her. But then, out of the corner of her eye, she glimpsed a figure coming towards them. Ben must have seen it, too, because he didn't touch her, even though she sensed he was angry enough to do so. Instead, he turned abruptly away and stalked off to meet his mother, leaving Cass to follow on legs that were distinctly weak.

CHAPTER EIGHT

CASS was dreaming, and in the dream she was swimming through layers of glittering blue water. She felt insubstantial, weightless, at one with the sea creatures who were swimming about her. The sunlight, streaming through the water above her, illuminated a magical world of waving fronds and rainbow-coloured fish, none of whom seemed to care that she was swimming beside them. They ignored her, carrying on about their business, with a total lack of curiosity. For her part, she could feel a distinct restriction in her nose, and her eyes felt vaguely sore. Her throat, too, felt most uncomfortable, and she guessed it was due to the choking lump of rubber she was holding between her teeth.

And then she realised what was happening. She was snorkelling. It was the mask she was wearing that was restricting her nose, and the rubber mouthpiece of the breathing tube was drying her throat. With a sudden twist of her body, she used the black flippers on her feet to propel herself towards the surface. But, as she struggled to break free from some constriction that was holding her down, the cool morning air, drifting in through her windows, brought a feathering of goose-flesh to her body. And, when she opened her eyes to the awareness that she was not snorkelling at all, but dreaming the whole thing, she discovered she had kicked off the single sheet, which had been all that was covering her.

It was a strangely disappointing discovery. For a few minutes, she had been totally convinced she was snorkelling, and although it hadn't always been an enjoyable experience it had been exciting. But she hadn't done any snorkelling since she was eighteen years old. Ben had taught her how to snorkel, and because of that, and the associations it provoked, she had always refused to participate whenever anyone else had invited her to try it. It had reminded her too strongly of that day at Calvado, and, although if she had tried it again it might have helped her to expunge the memories, she had never put it to the test.

She sighed now and, reaching for her watch, she looked at the time. It was barely six-thirty, far too early to get up, and yet she instinctively knew she would not go back to sleep again. The vividness of her dream had destroyed any hopes she might have had of drifting off again. Instead, all the haunting memories of that summer came flooding over her, and for once she didn't try to stem their flow…

At eighteen, Cass was tall and reasonably slim, and she wore her long pale hair in a single chunky braid. She was still a little shy, except with people she knew well, and although she attracted male eyes she had so far shown little interest in the opposite sex. She had been introduced to several eligible young men—Roger Fielding among them—whom her father considered suitable escorts, but her interest in them was negligible. She much preferred books and music to personal relationships, and, if her parents were disappointed at her lack of enthusiasm, they had only themselves to blame. For years, except when she was at boarding-school, she had been pretty much left to her own devices, expected to entertain herself, while Diana and Guido pursued their social ambitions. They had shown little regard for their daughter's needs as she was growing up, and it was unreasonable of them to expect her to behave like an extrovert when for most of her life she had lived an introverted existence. Cass was sweet-natured and generous with her affections, but she couldn't pretend to be something she was not, not even to please her father.

The only time she felt she really came alive was during the holidays she spent in Italy. In spite of Sophia Scorcese's attitude towards her, nothing could mar the excitement she felt at spending day after day in Ben's company, and sometimes, at the end of a holiday, she wondered how she would ever survive until the next year.

Of course, she occasionally saw Ben between times. Sometimes he came to England at his father's request, and once he attended a seminar in London, and stayed at Eaton Chare. One Easter, he had even spent two weeks in England, doing some research into medieval mysticism; but it wasn't the same. For one thing, her mother tended to commandeer his attention whenever she was around, and Cass had noticed how frequently Diana was around when Ben was in the house. In addition to which, she was prone to tell Cass to run along and do her homework whenever she attempted to involve Ben in conversation, and short of being rude to her mother there was little she could do.

But at Calvado she had him all to herself, at least for a good part of the time. And without her mother's daunting influence she was able to feel and act like an adult, and the fifteen years between them had never been a problem. On the contrary, Ben had always treated her like an equal, and although, as she grew older, her mother had protested that she really ought to spend her summers with them, her father had always been sympathetic when Cass had begged his support.

The year she had her eighteenth birthday, her father

bought the villa in Bermuda, and the whole household was going to spend the months of July and August on the island. 'You ought to come with us,' Diana told her daughter impatiently, the night before Cass was due to leave for Italy. 'Your father's invited the Hammonds, and Roger Fielding. And you know he's only going because he expects you to be joining us.'

'I'm going to Calvado, Mummy,' Cass insisted, in the process of choosing which cassette tapes she wanted to take with her. 'Signora Scorcese's expecting me. I can't change my mind now. It would be rude.'

'It's a damn sight more rude of you to spend every summer with that woman and her son, instead of with your own family,' returned her mother shortly. 'And don't pretend you really care what Sophia thinks. You're only going because of Ben!' She grimaced. 'You're so transparent, Cass. I'd have thought you'd have got over that schoolgirl crush by now!'

Cass's face had flushed scarlet at this accusation, but luckily the phone had rung at that moment and Diana had gone to answer it, negating any need for her to find an answer. All the same, her mother's words had disturbed her, promoting as they did images of her own reactions to Ben. And, like a self-fulfilling prophesy, they had lingered in her thoughts, so that what had happened had acquired a certain inevitability.

At the start of the holiday, however, she had no difficulty in putting such thoughts to the back of her mind. Ben had met her off the plane, as usual, at the international airport in Pisa, and to begin with she had been so delighted to be with him again that she had forgotten all about Diana's warning. She had so much to tell him, so many anecdotes about Diana and her father, and about her last term at school, that she hadn't noticed any particular tension between them. They were together again; she was happy, and that was all that mattered.

But in the days that followed the situation changed. It was almost imperceptible at first: a certain reluctance on her part to relinquish his hand after he had helped her up the cliff; an awareness of the lithe muscularity of his lean body; a curious willingness to follow him with her eyes, so that sometimes, when he turned about and caught her looking at him, she was overcome with embarrassment.

Initially, she thought Ben was unaware of her aberrations. He took her swimming and sightseeing as usual, and to all intents and purposes their relationship was exactly the same as it had been other years. He teased her just as much as he had ever done, and as he seldom seemed to take her seriously it wasn't too difficult to hide her feelings.

But slowly their relationship was changing. And she thought Sophia sensed it almost before Ben did himself. Certainly, the Italian woman seemed to realise the dangers in leaving them alone together. She found reasons for accompanying them everywhere, even making the arduous trek up from the cove on occasion, after spending an uncomfortable couple of hours under the beach umbrella. She drew the line at entering the water, but she kept a watching brief from the shoreline.

However, it was impossible for her to supervise them all the time. They often spent days away from the villa, exploring the Tuscan countryside, and swimming from quiet bays, far from the haunts of other tourists. Although Cass never forgave Ben for scaring her at the wheel of the powerful little Porsche, she became resigned to its terrifying turn of speed, and she was always a willing passenger. By this means, she became as familiar with the area around Calvado as Ben was himself.

But, in the curious way of fate, when disaster struck, it struck at Calvado and nowhere else. What happened could have happened at any one of a dozen beaches along the Ligurian coast, but it didn't. On all those occasions when she and Ben had been completely alone together, nothing untoward had occurred. In her memory, those days were filled with sun and sea and happiness, and nothing else. Whereas, what happened at Calvado had had all the trappings of a nightmare.

Was that why she had remembered it now? she wondered. Maybe that was why she had had the dream. Because it reminded her of the day she and Ben had gone snorkelling together, and of how she had got into difficulties. Certainly, she had no difficulty in remembering what had happened afterwards. The events of that morning were etched on her brain in images of fire.

It was such a silly thing she had done. For once, Sophia had not accompanied them down to the cove, and after spending perhaps fifteen minutes sunbathing on the beach Cass had suggested swimming across to the rocks at the other side of the bay, below the Benedictine abbey. It was quite a swim, but she knew the waters around the rocks were teeming with wildlife, and Cass was too restless to remain where she was. She wanted to swim; she wanted to burn off some of the surplus energy that was streaming through her veins like liquid oxygen. She wanted to test her strength until she was utterly exhausted. Maybe then she'd be able to relax, instead of living on the edge of emotional purgatory.

Ben had been reluctant to accompany her. He was quite content to lounge in the sun, one arm raised to protect his eyes from the glare, the other resting casually on his thigh. He looked so attractive lying there, she thought shamefully, his lean body bathed in a fine film of sweat. She didn't know exactly what she wanted, but the knowledge that he could be so indifferent to her feelings filled her with defiance.

'Are you coming?' she demanded, twisting her plait of hair up on to the top of her head and securing it with a comb. 'If you're too lazy to move, I shall go on my own. I can't lie here all morning. It's too—too boring!'

Ben groaned, and pushed himself up, sitting cross-legged on his towel. 'You're bored?' he echoed, squinting up at her. 'That's new, isn't it? As I recall it, you used to spend literally *hours* lying in the sun!'

Cass shrugged and reached for the face mask and breathing tube Ben had bought her. 'Perhaps I'm getting too old to lie on the beach,' she declared, ignoring his wry look of disbelief. 'In any event, I want some action. Are you coming, or aren't you? Make up your mind.'

'Well, you can't go on your own,' declared Ben flatly, getting to his feet, and she glared up at him.

'Why not? Don't you think I'm old enough?'

'Age has nothing to do with it,' he retorted, bending to pick up his own snorkelling equipment. 'OK. Let's go. Far be it from me to hold you back.'

It was a strenuous swim by any standards, and Cass had never attempted it before. The exploration they had once made of the rocks below the abbey had been achieved by circling the bay on foot, and entering the sea at Punta St Michel. Although she knew Ben had swum across the bay before, she had previously considered it was beyond her abilities, and half-way across she realised she wasn't going to make it. Her breathing was getting progressively laboured, and her legs were beginning to feel like lead. She badly wanted to turn back, but with Ben swimming strongly ahead of her she had to go on.

And then disaster struck. As she ploughed ever more

deeply into the waves, sometimes submerging her breathing tube completely, her lungs were suddenly filled with sea-water. Somehow, the valve on her breathing tube had become faulty and, unable to breathe, panic enveloped her.

She surged to the surface, threshing about wildly as she tore off her face mask and struggled to get some air. But the water in her lungs was weighing her down, and when Ben glanced back all he could see was a flailing vortex of arms and legs.

She never did get the opportunity to ask him what he had thought at that moment. But she did remember his face was grim as he swam back to her, and she was pretty sure that anger gave him the strength to get her back to the cove. Whatever, she coughed and choked all the way back, hardly able to kick her legs to keep herself afloat, relying completely on Ben's life-saving hold. And when he finally dragged her into the shallows he was absolutely exhausted. He barely staggered up out of the water before collapsing on the sand, and for a few minutes Cass was left to cope with her own recovery.

She had little doubt that Ben had saved her life. Had she been alone when the accident happened, she would never have been able to swim back to the shore. Even now, panting on the beach, her lungs burned with the aftermath of the water's invasion, and she had no strength left to climb the cliff.

When Ben stirred himself some minutes later, she was lying on her back with her eyes closed. For a moment, she guessed, he was half afraid she was unconscious, for he knelt beside her and cradled her face between hands that still shook from his ordeal, and said her name in a low, strangled voice.

'Cass,' he muttered. 'Oh, Cass! *Stai bene?*'

Her eyes opened as he spoke, and the expression he was wearing overwhelmed her. His lean face was dark with concern, and there was such a look of haunted anguish in his eyes that she lost all ability to hide what she was feeling.

'Oh, Ben,' she breathed, lifting her hand, and sliding her fingers into the damp vitality of his hair. And then, hardly aware of what she was doing, she brought his face down to hers.

He resisted for a moment, but only for a moment. When his lips touched hers, the control he had been exerting seemed to snap, and with a muffled groan he stretched his length beside her. The warm wetness of his body lay half over hers, his weight flattening her breasts between them, and his mouth had explored hers with ever-increasing urgency.

She sometimes used to wonder what would have happened if Sophia had not appeared as she had. For those mindless moments of time before his mother came striding across the sand and tore them apart, Ben had been totally lost to his emotions. It was only Sophia's intervention that had brought him to his senses, and her malevolent accusations had rung in Cass's ears for many years to come.

Of course, she had had to leave. At once. Sophia wouldn't allow her to stay in her house a moment longer than it took her to pack her bags, and, although he had said little, Cass had known Ben endorsed his mother's demands. He hadn't even driven her to the airport. A taxi had been summoned from Porto Camagio, and Cass's last view of the villa had been through the rear window of an ancient Fiat, with Sophia keeping a grim vigil in the garden.

The next few weeks had passed in a kind of dream. The

flight to Bermuda, the reckless way she had behaved with Roger, even her acceptance of his marriage proposal, had all been part and parcel of the emotional reaction she had suffered after the realisation of what she had done had really hit her. Her self-recrimination was crippling, and she felt sick every time she thought about what Ben must be thinking of her. He had always been so kind to her, so affectionate, never over-stepping the bounds of friendship, treating her with the tolerance of an older brother—which he was. But she had destroyed all that. She had taken his kindness—and Sophia's generosity—and thrown it in their faces. She had behaved abominably, and there were times when she truly wished she had died out there in the bay.

And then, when they returned to London, Ben came to see her.

She had already been wishing she had not accepted Roger's proposal, and when Ben appeared she had thought she was being given a chance to make her peace with him. She had been all prepared to accept the blame, to tell him it had all been her fault, and that she was so dreadfully sorry for the way she had behaved. But it hadn't happened like that.

She had been in her room when her mother had sent for her, and although, when she discovered that her mother was not alone, her initial reaction had been one of stunning relief, Ben's first words after Diana had left them had torn her hopes to shreds. He wasn't in London, as she had thought, to try and make peace between them. On the contrary, if anything his anger towards her seemed to have increased. He spent the next few minutes telling her what a spoilt, undisciplined, stupid little delinquent she was, and warning her to stay away from him from now on. He had been utterly unlike the Ben she was accustomed to, using words against her he had never used before, hurting her and humiliating her, until pride had revived her flagging spirit.

With a flourish, she had told him he was the stupid one, that he was making mountains out of molehills, that she hadn't given what happened a second thought. She also told him she was engaged to be married, and that he needn't flatter himself that she would be bothering him in future. She was going to be far too busy looking after her new husband.

After that, it had been a foregone conclusion that she would marry Roger. To back out would have been too humiliating and, besides, she had got a certain cruel satisfaction from sending Ben an invitation to the wedding. And he had come, much to her dismay. He had stood at the back of the church and listened to her make her vows to Roger, watching her walk down the aisle again afterwards with eyes that were curiously remote.

In the years that followed they had seen one another again, albeit infrequently. Cass had once accompanied Roger on a business trip to Genoa—at her father's suggestion—and Ben had been obliged to spend a couple of days with them. Not to do so would have inspired his father's antagonism, but Roger and Ben had never liked one another, and the exercise was not repeated.

Then, perhaps two years ago, Guido had invited Cass to join him on a trip he had to make to Florence, and they had stayed at the Villa Regina and spent several days with Ben.

But these were awkward occasions, at best. Ben saw to it that they were never alone together, and such conversation as they had was stilted, to say the least. The relationship they had once shared might never have been, and although there was no longer any animosity between them there was little sympathy either.

However, time had a habit of healing most things, and Cass's feelings towards Ben had always been ambivalent. Even when she told herself she hated him, she knew deep down inside her that it wasn't true. She couldn't hate Ben. He was too much a part of her; just as she had believed she was of him. And, as her marriage to Roger veered steadily on to the rocks, she had gradually come to believe that the only person who could help her was Ben. Those summers spent at Calvado had always seemed the happiest times of her life and, like an injured creature seeking a place to lick its wounds, she had returned to Italy, and the only man she had ever truly loved...

It was a damning admission, she knew, but as she thrust aside the covers and got out of bed her immortal soul meant less to her at that moment than the realisation that, once again, she was within a breath of losing everything.

It was three days since Ben had returned to the villa, but since that incident on the cliff path she had seen next to nothing of him. He was avoiding her, she knew: spending time with his mother, or working in the gardens with Carlo, refusing her invitations to go swimming, or driving, or simply to sunbathe on the terrace, with a chilling air of finality. He didn't want to be with her; he didn't even want to talk to her; he was immune behind the impregnable wall of his own invincibility.

For her part, Cass felt trapped, imprisoned, confined by the promise she had made Ben not to go down to the cove alone, yet unable to expunge her restless energies in any of the pursuits she loved. Oh, she had walked into the village a couple of times on errands for Maria, and no one objected to her spending all day, if she wished, exposing her body to the sun. But her mind was never at peace. She felt constantly at war with her conscience, and she was beginning to wonder just how much more she could take.

Stretching, she came to a decision. Even Ben's wrath was better than his indifference. She would not spend another day vegetating on the terrace. Whether he liked it or not, she was going to go swimming, and the only way he was going to stop her was by locking her in her room.

CHAPTER NINE

BEN was enjoying his second cup of coffee of the day when Cass came stalking on to the terrace. If he was surprised to see her, she was obviously equally surprised to see him, which wasn't so unusual as he had made a point during the last few days of being long gone before she put in an appearance. But today, for some reason, she had decided to get up at an earlier hour, and a quick glance at his watch reassured him that it was barely seven o'clock.

He got to his feet at once, partly out of politeness, partly out of a desire to put as much distance between them as possible, but he found to his annoyance that she wasn't prepared to let him go.

'Sit down,' she said tensely. 'I want to talk to you.' And, when he didn't immediately obey her, 'Or are you too much of a coward to hear what I have to say?'

The accusation was unwarranted, but he sensed a determination in her to get through the carefully erected wall of indifference with which he had surrounded himself. One way or another, she was going to have her way, and although he knew the dangers he told himself it would do no harm to listen.

With a muscle jerking in his cheek, he sank back into his chair, and he saw the sudden relief that crossed her face. Evidently, she had not been as sure of herself as he had thought. It was obvious she was living on her nerves, and his conscience stirred uneasily at his own unwilling guilt.

Crossing his ankle across his knee, he endeavoured to appear relaxed, but with her eyes on him it wasn't easy. Since she had put on a little weight, her beauty had become a vibrant torment, and he hoped the interview would not last long in his present state of awareness. The skimpy bra of her bikini was scarcely a suitable covering and, beneath the baggy Indian cotton trousers she was wearing over the briefs, her long legs displayed a honey-gold tan. She looked sophisticated, exotic and disturbingly sensual. A slender, grey-eyed Venus, with the face of an angel.

'Well?' he said after a moment, the edge to his voice an indication of his turmoil. 'What do you want?' He paused. 'I'm going out this morning, and I'd like to make an early start.'

'Going out?' she echoed, sinking into the chair opposite him, and gazing at him with anxious eyes. 'You mean— out? Or *away*? You're not going back to Florence! Oh, please, you can't.' She bit her lip. 'I won't let you.'

Ben sighed and, realising that if he wasn't careful Cass would raise her voice and waken his mother as well, he explained, 'I'm not going to Florence. Though,' he felt obliged to add, 'if that was my destination, I doubt that you could stop me. But, as it happens, I'm going to Verrazzino. My grandmother has been unwell and I'm going to visit her.' He shrugged. 'I'll probably be back tonight.'

'Take me with you!'

Resting her arms on the table, she was gazing at him appealingly, and Ben felt that stirring sense of guilt reassert itself. 'I can't.'

'Why can't you? You've never taken me to see your grandmother, and you know I'd like to meet her. Oh, please!' She stretched her hands across the table. 'Don't leave me here again.'

'Cass!'

His use of her name was a rebuke, and her shoulders sagged. 'Well,' she mumbled defensively, 'I won't spend another day lying in the sun. If you won't take me to Verrazzino, I'm going down to the cove.' She hunched her shoulders and then added her final thrust, 'I half wish someone would show up. At least that way I'd have someone to talk to.'

Ben felt his nerves clench. 'Don't be a fool!'

'What's foolish?' Cass gave him a resentful look. 'You've spent the last three days avoiding me, haven't you? The only company I get is at meal times, and then your mother makes sure she dominates the conversation.'

Ben sighed. 'You're not a child.'

'No, I'm not.'

'So you shouldn't need constant entertainment.'

'Constant entertainment?' She snorted. 'I don't get *any* entertainment!' She caught back a sob. 'I sometimes think you hate me. You obviously wish you'd never brought me here.' She sniffed. 'What's the matter? Has Daddy been getting on to you? Has he told you he holds you responsible for me leaving Roger? Well, if that's so, perhaps I ought to go back to London and be done with it. I've got to go sooner or later, and there's obviously no reason for me to stay here—'

'Calm down. *Calm down!*' With a feeling of helplessness, Ben captured the balled fists she was hammering soundlessly against the table, and smoothed his fingers over them. Then, with a weary sense of resignation, he added softly, 'I don't want you to go back to London. And—I definitely don't hate you.'

Slate-grey eyes, sparkling with unshed tears, gazed at him half disbelievingly. 'Don't you?'

'No.' Ben was certain about that. He regarded her steadily for a moment, and then gave in to an emotion stronger than himself. 'All right. Will I prove it if I take you to Verrazzino with me? Can you be ready in fifteen minutes? I'll buy you breakfast on the way.'

Cass's expression was incredible. 'Do you mean it?' she exclaimed. She was staring at him with her heart in her eyes, and he had to look away.

'I mean it,' he assured her roughly, withdrawing his hands from hers, and with a little cry of excitement she bounded to her feet.

'Just give me ten minutes,' she told him, touching her damp hair with an anxious hand and catching her lower lip between her teeth. 'And—thank you,' she added huskily, pausing at the entrance to the villa. 'I promise you, you won't regret it.'

Ben wished he could be as sure of that as he changed out of frayed denim shorts and a cotton vest into black jeans and a collarless shirt. He was doing something he had sworn he would never do, and he was perfectly aware of the risks he was taking. He knew Sophia would never forgive him, but some things just had to be done. Even if he had to spend the rest of his life living with her condemnation, he had to take Cass to meet *Nonna*. She deserved to know the truth, and he needed that absolution.

When Cass reappeared, she was sedately dressed in a button-through cotton dress and heeled sandals. Her hair had been dried and hung silky soft to her shoulders, the pale ends brushing the straps of the lemon yellow sundress. The tan she had acquired over these weeks had given her skin a golden luminescence, and only her eyes had received her attention: a dusky brush of umber mascara to darken the sun-bleached tips of her lashes.

'I'm ready,' she said, viewing his appearance with a disturbing candour, and Ben took a deep breath.

'So I see,' he allowed, indicating that she should precede him out of the door.

'I look all right, don't I?' she asked doubtfully, glancing back over her shoulder, evidently not sure what to make of his rather ironic comment, and he nodded.

'Most suitable,' he assured her drily, wondering what his grandmother would say when she discovered he had brought Guido Scorcese's daughter with him. 'Did you tell anyone where you were going?'

Cass looked discomfited. 'No.' She frowned. 'Do I have to?'

'I've told Maria,' Ben declared flatly, suddenly aware of his own duplicity. He should have told Sophia, he conceded with a pang. But that would have to wait. Right now, he needed to hang on to the conviction that what he was doing was justifiable. If Sophia had been involved, he might not have been able to sustain the will to defy her.

They drove south and west from Calvado, using the main *autostrada* to Livorno, before taking to less civilised roads. Ahead of them, the Apennines rose towards the deepening blue of the sky, while in the river valleys fields of corn and the silver-fringing of olive trees provided a striking contrast. The luxuriant landscape was dotted here and there with farms and villages, and terraces of vines climbed up the hillsides to medieval towns that looked like fortresses.

There was a certain timelessness about the area; a feeling that the people who lived here didn't much care what went on in the outside world. Life moved more slowly; there was time to appreciate good food and fine wine; the family was still the most important social factor, and the preponderance of children they saw in the villages seemed to signify their determination to perpetuate the custom.

Ben had stopped at a service area on the motorway so that Cass could get some breakfast, and he stopped again at a small *ristorante* overlooking the valley of a winding river soon after twelve o'clock.

'We're about thirty miles from Verrazzino,' he told her, after the waiter had seated them on a terrace overlooking the gorge. 'But I think it's wiser if we don't arrive until after lunch. If *Nonna* has been ill, she doesn't deserve to be troubled by two extra mouths to feed.'

'Of course not.' Cass gave him a rather uncertain smile. 'You're not regretting inviting me, are you?'

Ben's mouth turned down slightly at the corners. 'I thought you invited yourself,' he remarked teasingly, and saw the becoming colour enter her cheeks at his words.

'You know what I mean,' she murmured, taking an inordinate interest in the raffia place-mat, and he had to smile.

'No,' he said, causing her to glance up at him a little doubtfully. 'No, I'm not regretting inviting you. It can be a lonely drive.'

Cass relaxed. 'Well, you haven't said much on the way here,' she remarked with more confidence. And then, as if realising her words could be misconstrued, she added hurriedly, 'Not that I mind. I've been fascinated by the scenery.'

'Yes.' Ben lay back on the wooden bench. 'It is beautiful, isn't it? When I was younger, I used to wish we lived here.'

Cass frowned. 'But—both Daddy and your mother came from this area, didn't they?'

'Oh, yes.' Ben breathed a little heavily. 'As a matter of fact, the Scorceses used to own a lot of land around here. Guido was the local—what would you say?—squire's son? Whereas Sophia's origins were much less grand. My grandparents used to work in the Scorcese vineyards.'

'Did they? You never told me that!' Cass arched brows that were several shades darker than her hair. 'How romantic! Do you think they were very much in love?'

Ben shook his head abruptly, half wishing he hadn't started this, and the arrival of the waiter to take their order gave him the opportunity he needed. But after their spaghetti had been served, and a carafe of house wine was sparkling on the table between them, Cass turned again to the subject of his childhood. Short of being rude and alienating her once again, he had little choice but to answer her questions.

'Doesn't it surprise you that you were an only child?' she ventured, and, looking into her eyes, he wondered what she was really thinking. She must know, as well as he did, that their relationship had gone far beyond the bounds of sibling affection, and asking him about his family was only a precarious diversion.

But it was safer to keep their conversation in these fairly impersonal channels, and, applying himself to his spaghetti, he said casually, 'I might say the same of you.'

'Oh—' She grimaced now. 'Mummy couldn't have any more children after I was born. Or that's her story, anyway. But, Sophia didn't have that problem, did she? It would be rather a coincidence if she did.'

'No.' Ben considered his words before continuing, 'No, she didn't have any problems that I know of.' He hesitated a moment, and then proceeded evenly, 'And I do have lots of cousins. An occupational hazard of this area, I'm afraid.'

Cass caught her breath. 'I wouldn't call it a hazard.'

'Wouldn't you?' Ben spoke without expression, not trusting himself to look at her.

'No.' Cass took another deep breath. 'As a matter of fact, I'd like to have children. I think it must be lovely to have lots of brothers and sisters.'

Ben concentrated on his spaghetti. 'With Roger?' he enquired tightly, and he heard her shivering sigh.

'No. Not with Roger,' she told him definitely. And then, 'I probably won't ever have a family. I've no intention of getting married again.'

Ben despised himself for the sense of relief he felt at her words, but he forced himself to make one final comment. 'Not all men are like Roger,' he stated flatly. 'You can't possibly know you won't meet a man some day who you will want to marry, and then—'

'I do know,' she interrupted him tremulously, her voice an octave higher than it was before. Then, as if realising she was attracting attention, she lowered it again before saying, 'You know I won't marry anyone else. I shouldn't have married Roger in the first place.'

The conviction in her voice was unmistakable, and Ben cursed himself anew for the satisfaction he felt at hearing her denounce her marriage. She was so intense, so passionate, yet so innocent in some ways, in spite of the years she had lived with Fielding. Imagining her with that insensitive oaf inspired an almost primitive rage inside him. He would have liked nothing so much as to beat Roger to within an inch of his life. And it didn't help to know that at least half his anger came from his own sense of impotence, the knowledge that it was his own frustration tearing him apart as much as the other man's existence.

They were silent for a while and Ben, finding some difficulty in swallowing his own food, discovered that Cass was having a similar problem. However, he refrained from commenting on the obvious, and after pouring her more wine he began to tell her a little about the history of his country. It was a subject with which he was infinitely more familiar, and he made his words as entertaining as possible. He told her about the hill town of Volterra, with its medieval palaces; he described the tiny republic of San Marino, situated in rocky splendour on Monte Titano; and he recounted the tale of the church built over St Francis's oratory at Santa Maria degli Angeli, where the roses in the gardens were said to be thornless, ever since a famous act of penance by the saint.

By the time their coffee was served after the meal, the atmosphere between them was considerably lighter, and Ben was able to lean back and enjoy Cass's company without the gut-wrenching pull of emotion. He was almost able to convince himself that he had just brought her along for company, but not quite. In the deeper recesses of his mind, he knew it wasn't true. His purpose was just as sharp as ever.

It was nearly half-past two when they reached Verrazzino. The final phase of their journey had been much slower because of the narrower roads, and Ben knew Cass would have liked to stop on the way and explore more of the countryside. Wooded slopes, thickly spread with gorse and heather, gave way to a gentle valley where the river they had seen from the terrace of the *ristorante* meandered lazily through fields of ripening corn. There was a smell of pine and citrus, and the lake, where Ben told her he had once swum as a child, opened into its cypress-shaded basin, as green and inviting now as it had been all those years ago.

There were children playing among the trees and splashing in the water, and Cass propped her chin on the arm she was resting on her open window, watching them enviously as they drove by. The sleek flash of their brown bodies must have reminded her of when Ben had caught her swimming three days ago, and, giving him a teasing look, she said, 'Didn't you wear a bathing suit either?'

But Ben didn't rise to the bait. 'Bathing suits were in short supply in Verrazzino,' he replied indifferently. 'By the time I was old enough to notice, Guido had gone to live in England, and my mother never came here again.'

Cass's white teeth imprisoned her lower lip for a moment. 'But why?' she exclaimed. 'I would have thought— that is—well, that she would have needed her family.'

'No.' Ben shook his head, and then, glimpsing her troubled expression, he smiled. 'Don't look so worried. Sophia didn't need their support. Your father took care of her financially, and pride did the rest.'

'But—you must have missed your cousins.'

'I suppose I did.' Ben was philosophical. 'Perhaps that's why I worked harder at the academy. I didn't have the distractions of other boys my age.'

'Oh, Ben!'

Cass's eyes were full of sympathy now, but Ben chose to ignore them. 'We're almost there,' he said instead, and to his relief she turned back to the window.

Verrazzino was typical of the villages of the area. There was the inevitable church, with its gothic bell-tower; a neat little inn, advertising the wholesome Italian food it served; and a cluster of cottages around a flower-strewn *piazza*, where children and dogs played with a distinct disregard for traffic.

'Is this it?' Cass was impressed. 'Isn't it pretty?'

'Pretty primitive,' remarked Ben drily, parking the car in the square, and hoping one of the ubiquitous footballs that were flying around wouldn't dent the Porsche's bodywork. 'We can walk from here. It's just a few metres.'

Cass slid out eagerly, her pale beauty immediately drawing attention to their arrival. When Ben thrust open his door and got out, too, he was instantly hailed by at least half a dozen people who recognised him, and were curious about his companion, and he responded to their *come stas* and *come vas* with rueful resignation.

'Have you come to see your grandmother?' asked one enormously fat woman who came ambling across to them, and Ben nodded.

'That's right, Marina. Is she any better?'

'She will survive,' replied the woman carelessly, her attention focused on Cass's sun-warmed face. 'Who is this, Benvenuto? Your betrothed? Or your wife? She is very beautiful. And she looks at you so adoringly!'

Ben could feel the heat invading his own face at that moment, and, realising Cass could understand at least a part of what Marina was saying, he knew he had to reply. 'Er—this is Cassandra—um—Scorcese,' he introduced her stiffly. And then, in English, 'Cass, this is Marina Pisano. She is married to my cousin Luigi.'

'*Molto lieta, signora,*' Cass murmured politely, giving Ben a curious look, and Marina's thick fingers encased her hand.

'*Buona sera*, Cassandra,' she murmured, surveying the girl with a speculative gaze. 'Welcome to Verrazzino.'

'Thank you. I mean—*grazie*.'

Cass was looking embarrassed now and, sliding his fingers around her wrist, Ben intervened. 'You will excuse us, won't you?' he averred smoothly. 'We want to see *Nonna*, and we have to drive back tonight.'

'You are not staying?'

Marina was evidently loath to waste her opportunities, but Ben began to walk away, taking Cass with him. 'Not on this occasion,' he assured her firmly. '*A piu tardi. Ciao!*'

'Why didn't you tell her I was your sister?' Cass asked

as they turned into a narrow lane off the square, where the cottages opened directly on to the pavement. She coloured. 'Because she said I was in love with you?'

'She didn't say that,' retorted Ben tersely, halting in front of a narrow house, with tubs of fuchsias and geraniums flanking the open door. 'Anyway, here we are. This is my grandmother's cottage.'

It was just three rooms really, with an attic room upstairs, where they stored food, and blankets for the winters, which could be cold in this part of Tuscany. But it was spotlessly clean. Ben knew his grandmother had borne nine children in these small rooms, two of whom had died, and seven who would likely live to survive her. He used to love coming here, playing with his cousins, pretending he was one of them. It was strange really, because he actually had belonged here, but it was years before he knew it; and by then it was too late.

Lucia Pisano was sitting in a high-backed chair in the room that served as a kitchen, and was situated at the back of the house. In spite of the heat of the day, she had several shawls draped about her shoulders, and although she was evidently in some pain her eyes were as indomitable as ever.

'*Benvenuto!*' she exclaimed when he appeared in the doorway, and casting her shawls aside she tried to get out of her chair.

But Ben forestalled her, striding quickly across the floor to kneel at her feet, taking her gnarled hands between his strong palms, and raising his face for her kiss. '*Nonna,*' he said, his smile for her warm and tender. 'It's so good to see you again.'

'For me, also.' Lucia withdrew her hands from his to cup his lean face with loving fingers. 'Sophia said in her letter that you might come, but I know what a busy man you are.'

'Not too busy for you, *Nonna*,' he assured her, getting to his feet again with some reluctance, as out of the corner of his eye he saw Cass hovering in the doorway. His grandmother saw Cass, too, as he moved out of her line of vision, and her eyes widened uncomprehendingly, requiring an explanation. 'I—this is Cass—*Cassandra*,' he volunteered, as he had done before. 'I hope you don't mind me bringing her with me. I—wanted her to meet you.'

Lucia gave him a questioning look. 'Cassandra?' she echoed, in a faint voice. 'You mean—this is Guido Scorcese's daughter?'

'Yes.' Ben took Cass's distinctly anxious fingers in his and drew her forward. 'Cass, this is my grandmother—Lucia Pisano.'

Cass took the hand the old lady held out and made a polite response. But it was obvious she had taken his grandmother's startled words to mean something else, and Ben guessed she was associating her attitude with Sophia's.

'She is a beautiful girl,' Lucia said now, as Cass stood somewhat awkwardly beside him. 'I am very pleased to meet you, Cassandra. You do not know this, but I have wanted to meet you for a very long time.'

The old lady spoke in Italian, and Ben glanced at Cass to see if she understood. She seemed to, but she still looked a little anxious, and taking her wrist between his fingers he applied what he hoped was a reassuring pressure.

'Don't worry,' he said, speaking in English now. '*Nonna* likes you.'

Cass was breathing rather unevenly. He could hear it.

And her eyes, when she looked at him, were still full of doubt. 'Um—Sophia is her daughter,' she mumbled, low enough so that only he could hear, and he wished they were alone.

'*Nonna's* not Sophia,' he told her softly. 'Now, sit down and relax. It's going to be all right.'

'You must be hungry,' said Lucia suddenly as Cass subsided into a basketwork chair, and Ben quickly enlightened her.

'We had lunch at Monte Giorgio,' he told her gently, ignoring her automatic protest. 'We didn't want to put you to any trouble, *cara*. Besides,' he glanced at Cass, 'we weren't very hungry. We'll get a meal on our way back tonight, so don't worry about us.'

'Then you must have some wine. I insist,' declared the old lady, evading his hands to take a bottle of the rich red vintage of the area from her shelves. 'There, in that cupboard, Benvenuto, you will find some glasses. We cannot allow Guido Scorcese's daughter to visit us without offering her any refreshment.'

'Oh, really—' began Cass, recognising the fact that her relationship to her father was being mentioned again, but Ben silenced her.

'It's OK,' he said, half impatiently, following his grandmother's instructions and taking three rather fine glasses from the cupboard. He uncorked the bottle himself and poured the wine. '*Salute,*' he added, raising his glass to theirs. His lips twisted. 'A fine wine drunk in fine company.'

He watched Cass as she sipped her wine, and felt a dark renewal of his frustration. He had brought her here, he acknowledged bitterly. He had introduced her to *Nonna*. And what now? He expelled a heavy breath. He couldn't do it. He couldn't say what he had intended to say, and live with his conscience.

He caught his grandmother's eyes upon him, and moved abruptly away. The need for absolution was almost overwhelming, but at what price? He needed to get out of the house. He needed to get away from the awful web of deception that still held him in its choking grip. He had thought that by coming here he could expunge his guilt, but he couldn't. This was his problem, and his alone. He couldn't involve *Nonna* in his miserable plight.

CHAPTER TEN

CASS didn't know what to do. Ben had gone outside and left her sitting with the old lady, and it would have been rude of her to get up and follow him. All the same, she thought it was rather inconsiderate of him to abandon her in this way. Particularly as her knowledge of Italian was comparatively limited, and his grandmother didn't appear to have a single word of English.

Exchanging a rather nervous smile with Lucia, she looked uneasily around the small kitchen, searching for something to distract the old lady's attention. A pair of photographs in a leather frame, standing on the white-washed dresser, caught her eye, and with a murmured, *'Chi é questo?'* she got up from her chair and crossed the room.

She saw at once that it was a picture of Ben and his mother, a younger Ben, with, surprisingly, a dark moustache. She shook her head. She couldn't ever remember seeing Ben with a moustache, but she supposed it was possible he had grown one once. After all, there had been long intervals of time when she hadn't seen him. All the same, he did look to be in his early twenties in the picture, and as far as she remembered he had been at university in England at that time. Hadn't he?

Suddenly becoming aware that Lucia was watching her, she coloured. Then, turning with the photographs still in her hands, she murmured awkwardly, 'Um—Ben—Benvenuto *é sua madre, no? Lui era molto giovane!*'

'No, signora.' The old lady shook her head, and then,

146

as if realising Cass didn't comprehend her meaning, she added in poor, but perfectly understandable, English, 'Is not Benvenuto. Is—how you say?—*il figlio di mio fratello, capisce?*'

Cass blinked. 'You mean—your nephew?'

'Ah, *sì.*' Lucia nodded. 'Nephew, yes. Is handsome, no?'

'Is handsome, yes,' said Cass ruefully, setting the frame back on the dresser. It had disturbed her, seeing Ben's image so closely reflected in the face of a cousin. A cousin once removed, at that, she amended silently. She wondered why Ben had never mentioned the resemblance. After all, it was unusual.

'Come,' said Lucia abruptly, breaking into her thoughts. 'Sit.' Evidently, she knew more of Cass's language than she had thought. 'Speak of Benvenuto.'

'Of Benvenu—' Cass broke off. 'I don't understand. *Non capisco!* What can I tell you?'

Lucia's veined hands gathered her shawl more closely about her. 'Is well?' she asked encouragingly. 'Is happy?'

Cass moistened her dry lips, wishing Ben would come back. But he didn't, and she had to answer. 'I—think so,' she murmured. 'Um—yes.'

Lucia regarded her consideringly. 'You stay Sophia, no?'

'What? Oh—yes.'

'Benvenuto also?'

'At the moment.' Cass nodded, in case her words were unfamiliar. 'For a few days, at least.'

'*Bene, bene.*' The old lady lay back in her chair. 'Sophia—she knows you come here?' She pointed the floor.

Cass shook her head now, and cast an anxious look over her shoulder. Where was Ben? Why didn't he come back?

'*Il suo padre*—' Lucia was speaking again, and Cass had to listen to her, '—he send you?'

'To Italy? No.' Cass sighed. 'But, well—I've been ill. I needed a holiday.'

'*E che di suo marito?* Your—husband. Is not with you?'

'No.' Cass wondered how many questions she was going to ask, but she decided she had to be honest. 'I—I've left him.'

'Ah.' Lucia's dark eyes, so like her grandson's, glittered. 'You come—to Benvenuto, *si*?'

Cass wondered if her face could possibly look as red as it felt. 'I—suppose so,' she admitted uncomfortably.

'*E*—you care for Benvenuto?'

Cass sighed. 'Naturally.'

'*Naturale?*' echoed her companion softly. She paused. 'You love him!'

Cass gulped. 'Well—he is—he is my brother.'

There was silence for a few moments, and Cass stared out into the brilliant sunlight until her eyes were blind in the shadows of the room. Her brother! she thought unsteadily. But she had never treated him like a brother. Was that obvious to Lucia? Was it obvious to anyone else?

'I—I wonder where Ben has gone,' she ventured at last, forced to say something to break the uneasy silence, but Lucia seemed as absorbed with her thoughts as she had been until her conscience got in the way. 'Um—I expect we'll have to be leaving soon. It's such a long drive back.'

'Is not true,' said Lucia suddenly, and Cass stared at her in confusion.

'Oh, it is,' she assured her confidently. 'It took us almost five hours to—'

'No. No!' Lucia waved her hands impatiently. 'No kilometres! *Il suo fratello!* Your *brother*! Benvenuto is not your brother!'

In spite of his earlier contention of leaving before dinner, it was after eight o'clock before Ben was allowed to depart. He had returned, accompanied by two of his cousins, and their wives and families, and in the resulting confusion it was easy for him to avoid her eyes.

Besides, everyone wanted to meet her and talk to her, and the wine flowed freely as reminiscences were exchanged. The children, particularly the girls, hung about her chair, admiring her sandals and her hair and the simple gold bangle she wore on her arm. They all wanted to try it on, and even the youngest, a baby of no more than eighteen months, crawled up her skirts and settled in her lap.

Yet, for all their kindness, Cass couldn't wait to leave. The things Ben's grandmother had told her, the amazing story she had told about Francesco—*Ben's real father*—and Sophia, and Guido, couldn't wait to be related. And it was a hundred times more annoying because Ben seemed totally immune to her signals.

A simple meal was prepared, and although food was the last thing on Cass's mind she felt obliged to eat a little. Actually, the spicy *bolognese* and newly baked bread was very tasty, and despite her agitation she managed to eat her share. The food helped to ease the growing feeling of excitement in her stomach. It helped to calm her nerves and slow her racing pulse.

Ben, however, ate little. Aware of him with every nerve in her body, Cass seldom took her eyes off him, and if anyone else besides his grandmother noticed, she didn't much care. *Oh, Ben,* she fretted silently, *what did they do to you?* The secret he had harboured all these years had almost destroyed their lives.

At last Ben was forced to say his farewells. It was almost dark, and when several members of the family accompanied them back to where they had left the car moths and other flying insects hummed about their ears. There were one or two derisive comments about the Porsche, but they were made and accepted in good part, and Ben embraced each of his cousins in turn before climbing behind the wheel. Cass came in for her own share of hugging, particularly from the children, and on impulse she gave the eldest girl her bangle, refusing to take it back again when the girl's mother demurred.

'Please,' she said, *'per favore, non importa!'* and she made a dismissing gesture it would have been rude to contradict.

'Grazie, grazie!'

The Italian woman thanked her politely enough, but as they drove out of the square Ben's reaction was furious. 'Don't you realise, you embarrassed Gina there?' he demanded, cornering too fast and sending a solitary hen squawking into the ditch. 'These people can't afford to throw expensive gold bracelets around as presents! What will Maria do with it? Her mother won't let her wear it, and it's not much use for anything else.'

Cass caught her breath, the urgency she had felt to talk to Ben alone evaporating in a cloud of indignation. 'She could always *sell* it!' she retorted, hunching herself into the farthest corner of her seat. 'What a fuss to make, for heaven's sake! Isn't gold a good enough currency for your precious Italian relatives?'

Ben's face was dark with anger. 'You will not speak of my family in that contemptuous way!' he snapped.

'The Pisanos are a fine and respected family in Verraz-zino. I'm proud to be one of them.'

'I'm sure you are.' Cass made the remark in the same defiant tone, and Ben glared at her.

'What is that supposed to mean?' he countered. 'Aren't they good enough for you? Is that what you're trying to say?'

'No, of course not.' Cass was angry at his summary assumption. 'I liked them. I liked them all. You know I did. And I'm sorry if you think I acted stupidly. I just wanted to do something to show my thanks.'

'Yes. Well—' Ben's temper gradually subsided. 'I suppose I did rather over-react, didn't I?' He ran a somewhat weary hand through his hair, and massaged the muscles at the back of his neck. 'What can I say? I guess I'm tired. It has been a long, hot day, and I could surely do with a shower.'

Cass straightened in her seat. 'Then—let's stop at the lake,' she suggested tentatively. 'We could—go for a swim. As this is a day for reminiscences, why don't you remind yourself of one more?'

'Don't be crazy!' Ben's voice was grim once more. 'It's far too late to go swimming. Even if I wanted to do so, which I don't.'

Cass sighed. 'It was only a suggestion.'

'A stupid one!'

'If you say so.' She shrugged. 'It was you who said you were hot and needed a shower, not me.'

'Oh, grow up, Cass, will you?' Ben expelled an impatient breath. 'Who in their right mind is going to go swimming in a lake at this time of night, just because they're feeling *hot*?'

'It's not late.'

'Forget it!'

Cass bent her head. 'Lovers might.'

'We're not lovers,' he retorted savagely.

'We could be,' she ventured, her voice barely audible, but he heard her, and with a violent movement he swung the car off the road and brought it to a shuddering standstill.

'I should have let Roger choke you, do you know that?' he snarled, his face in the light from the dash almost demoniacal in his fury. 'What the hell do you mean by making a remark like that? What in hell are you trying to do to me? My mother warned me that you were trouble, but fool that I was, I insisted on helping you anyway.' He took a deep breath. 'Well—it's over, Cass. You can pack your bags and leave in the morning. Find yourself another protector! I've had it as far as you're concerned.'

Cass was trembling after this outburst. Had she been wrong? she wondered dazedly. Had his grandmother been wrong? Did Ben know that he wasn't Guido Scorcese's son, or didn't he? The way he was looking at her now, she wasn't prepared to gamble.

Without making any response, she fumbled and found the handle of the door, pushing it open and scrambling out before he could stop her. Through the trees she could see the glimmer of something that looked like water, and as she stumbled away from the car she realised what it was. Inadvertently, Ben had stopped the car only yards from the lake where the children had been swimming earlier in the day. And whether he liked it or not, she decided, she was going to dip her toes in the water. He needed time to cool off, and she was going to give it to him. After the tongue-lashing she had just endured, she deserved a moment's respite to recover.

'Cass! Cass, where the hell do you think you're going?' As she made off between the trees, she heard Ben open his door and call her name. But he didn't sound any the less furious, so she didn't bother to answer. She was still hurt and angry herself over what he had said to her, and the idea that tomorrow she might be on her way back to England filled her with dismay. It couldn't be true. The wild excitement she had felt when his grandmother had relayed her story couldn't just sputter and die like a spent candle. If Ben didn't know, she had to tell him. She couldn't face the thought of living her life now without the man she loved.

The still waters of the lake confronted her, edged with reeds, and silvery in the light of the rising moon. It was a beautiful spot, the trees dark and protective, the grass lush and green beneath her feet. Even in the dark it held no terrors for her, locked as she was in the troubled prison of her thoughts. What was she going to do? What could she do? she fretted. Did she really have the right to break a confidence? Did she really know that Ben shared her feelings?

For all her avowed sense of bravado, she started violently when she heard a footfall behind her on the grass. Glancing over her shoulder, her face showed up stark and white in the moonlight, and the man who had stalked her to the lakeside admitted his defeat.

'It's me,' he muttered harshly, stepping closer to her, so that she could feel the heated draught of his breath against her sensitised skin. He shook his head as she relaxed, and turned to look at the water. 'So—you found the lake, after all. I should have known better than to argue with you. You usually get your own way.'

'Do I?' Cass's voice was husky. 'Do I, Ben?' She paused. 'Does that mean you're going to come swimming with me, after all?'

Ben's breathing was uneven as he turned to look at her

again. 'You're not going swimming in there,' he said flatly.

'Why not?'

'Because you're not.'

'That's not an answer,' she declared, kicking off her sandals. 'Hmm, doesn't the grass feel good between your toes?'

'*Cass!*' His control was slipping; she could sense it. But whether it was slipping into passion, or simply into anger, she didn't dare to speculate.

Stepping to the edge of the grass, where a thin wedge of shingle was lapped by gentle waves, she dipped her toe. 'Oh, it's cold!' she exclaimed, skipping back on to the grass again. 'But so soft,' she added. 'I bet it feels like silk against your skin.'

'You're not going to find out,' retorted Ben grimly, grabbing for her arm, but she managed to evade him.

'You can't stop me,' she taunted, her fingers going to the bootlace straps of her dress and sliding them off her shoulders. 'Come on, don't be a spoilsport! Wouldn't you like to take off those tight, uncomfortable—*clothes*?'

The word she had almost used was implicit in the sentence, and Ben swore; rather colourfully, Cass felt. 'This isn't going to make me change my mind,' he told her balefully. 'All you're doing is just reinforcing the opinion I had already formed of you. Now, are you ready to go back?'

Cass's fingers stilled, all the reckless excitement going out of her actions. Pushing the straps back up on to her shoulders, she tried instead to regulate her breathing. What was it she had read once: if you can control your breathing, you can control yourself? Something like that, anyway, she acknowledged dully. One of those silly little bits of information you clung to at times like these.

'Shall we go?'

Ben's voice was almost that of a stranger, and she looked at him in the pale light, wondering if he really despised her as much as he seemed to. This had been going to be such a marvellous evening, she sniffed, despising herself for once more giving way to tears. Was it only giving away the bangle that had caused everything to go so wrong?

'Ben...' she began tremulously, stalling when she should have been putting on her sandals, and he groaned.

'Not now, Cass.'

'Yes, now,' she insisted, wiping a recalcitrant tear from her cheek. 'Do you—do you really hate me?'

'I don't hate you.' Ben raked his hair with brutal fingers. 'For pity's sake, Cass, I've never said I hated you. We're just not—not compatible, that's all. Let's just leave it at that.'

Cass's tongue circled her lips. 'And you're not angry with me?'

'Oh, what is this?' Ben rolled his eyes skyward. 'Of course I'm angry with you. You say crazy things, and you make me *do* crazy things! Why shouldn't I be angry? Don't you think I have reason?'

He turned back towards the car, but still Cass stood her ground. 'I used to think you cared about me,' she persisted, kicking uselessly at a clump of turf. 'I used to think you loved me—'

'Oh, Cass!' This time, the way he said her name was anguished. As he looked across the width of the clearing towards her, she could see that at last she had penetrated his defensive shell. 'I do love you,' he muttered harshly, coming back to her on leaden feet. 'But we both know the futility of that, don't we? So why don't you come on back to the car and stop tormenting both of us?'

Cass took a quivering breath. 'Because—because I know you're not my brother!'

Ben stared at her with haggard eyes. 'What?'

'I—I know you're not my brother,' repeated Cass unsteadily, wondering as she said the words if he really knew the truth. 'Your—your grandmother told me. About—about how your real father was killed when he found an unexploded shell that had been buried since the end of the last war; how—how your mother married my father because she discovered she was pregnant.' She paused expectantly. 'Your grandmother said you knew about it. You did, didn't you? Oh, Ben, stop looking at me like that! You don't know how much this means to me. For goodness' sake, tell me how you feel. Tell me it's not—not a lie!'

'It's not a lie.'

But Ben wasn't jumping up and down and cheering the way she would have expected him to do—*the way she felt like doing*. What was wrong? Why wasn't he glad she knew the truth? It explained so many things, not least her own uncontrollable attraction towards him. It wasn't some awful incestuous need, it was simply an instantaneous recognition of the man she loved, *had always loved*.

Putting out a hand, she touched his sleeve, but he drew back from her overture with unflattering haste. 'Don't,' he said abruptly, the one word dashing all Cass's hopes. 'I don't know how else to say this, but it doesn't—it can't—make any difference to us.'

Cass gasped. 'Don't be ridiculous! Of course it does.'

'No.' He was adamant.

Cass gazed at him blankly. 'Why not?' She spread her hands again, this time in a rather bemused gesture. 'Unless—unless you didn't mean what you said just now. Forgive me if I seem a little confused, but didn't you just tell me you loved me? Or was that an attempt to get me to go back to the car? A sort of carrot to appease my pride?'

'Don't be silly.'

Ben spoke wearily, but Cass was too het up now to try and understand what he was trying to say. Her world seemed to be falling to pieces around her, and all she was suddenly thinking was how wonderful it would be to sink beneath the waters of the lake.

'I'm not silly,' she exclaimed now, tearing the straps of her dress off her shoulders again, and pushing it down over her hips. Then, as Ben watched in shocked disbelief, she removed her silk panties and, turning, plunged into the water, so that by the time he had comprehended what was happening she was several yards out from the shore.

The water was briefly numbing, the trees that shaded its banks ensuring that it never reached the temperature of the sea. As she kicked out into deeper water, she thought it might be quite easy to drown. All she had to do was let the water chill her; her frozen limbs would probably do the rest.

'Cass!'

Ben's hoarse summons was a brief diversion. He had come to stand on the shingle that sloped down to the water, and even from this distance, and given the poor light, she could still sense his grim frustration.

'Cass,' he called again, as she drifted further from his reach. 'Cass, for heaven's sake, get out of there! We need to talk. I realise that. Maybe I didn't react very positively to what you said just now, but that was because I was stunned. Come on! At least give me a chance to explain. For goodness' sake, stop playing games?'

Games? Cass felt the bitter tears well up again. He actually thought this was a game! He had no conception of how she felt; no idea at all of how much he had hurt her. He assumed this was just her way of paying him back. That when she'd tired of keeping him waiting, she'd come out of the water again, and go with him. Did he honestly believe that what she had learned could simply be disregarded? Did he really expect her to go on with her life as if everything was just as before?

'Cass, don't go any further!' she heard him yell warningly, but she paid him no attention. What did it matter what he said? she asked herself poignantly. She didn't care if the water was too cold, or there were currents she didn't know about. She didn't want to live, in any case. She wanted to die. It would be a definite advantage if he had to stand there and watch her suffer. A kind of rough justice for the injuries he had invoked.

'Cass, for heaven's sake!'

But it was too late for him to feel any remorse, she told herself severely. He had had his chance, and he had thrown it away. There wouldn't be any more intimate dinners or nights spent dancing under the stars. He would never again be able to hold her in his arms and bruise her mouth with kisses. And she would never run her fingers through his hair...

The painful—yet strangely hypnotic—dreams were abruptly interrupted. Her lazily moving legs were suddenly trapped in ropes of waving weed, and when she tried to kick herself free the weed only wound itself more strongly about her.

She came upright with a start, threshing about in the water as she struggled to escape the clinging tendrils, and, although moments before she had told herself she wanted to die, now she was literally fighting for her life. A dread panic gripped her at the thought that perhaps her wishes were to be granted.

Dear God, what was she going to do? she choked, finding herself underwater with the ghastly weed in her mouth. She was at least a couple of hundred yards away from the shore, with no earthly chance of being within her depth. The quiet lake which moments before had seemed a peaceful haven was now a place of violence and terror. She was unhappy, it was true, desperate even, but she didn't want to die. So long as Ben was alive, surely she could always hope...

CHAPTER ELEVEN

'KEEP still!'

The strong, reassuring voice was blessedly familiar. As her limbs obeyed his harsh command, Ben swiftly tore her free of the strangling weed. Then, pushing her towards the shore, he swam smoothly after her. Within minutes she had reached the shingle, and staggered up on to the grassy bank. But, once there, her legs gave out on her, and she collapsed on to the turf, uncaring of her shameful lack of covering.

'You—you saved my life,' she stammered, hearing Ben come up out of the water after her, and presently his lean length dropped down beside her.

'As long as you don't make a habit of it,' he remarked drily, leaning on his elbows beside her. He panted. 'Hell, I must be out of condition. I thought I wasn't going to make it.'

Cass looked at him then, his bare shoulders gleaming in the moonlight. He had evidently shed his shirt and trousers before diving into the water, and his skin looked smooth and muscled beneath its damp film of hair.

'I—I don't know what to say,' she murmured. 'I'm sorry.'

'Yes. So you should be.' He breathed heavily. 'I did try to warn you.'

'But—the children we saw earlier—'

'Don't swim out as far as you did. In any case, we were always warned about the reeds.' He grimaced. 'You gave me a scare!'

Cass expelled a sigh. 'What can I say? I suppose it just reinforced your opinion of me.'

'What else?' he muttered, but his eyes were moving from her face, over the downy curves of her body. Her nipples, already sharply defined by the cold water, seemed to harden beneath his gaze, and when his eyes dropped to the shadowy triangle of hair between her legs her whole being trembled.

'Oh, hell!' he groaned, looking away, but Cass was too aroused to let him leave her.

'Touch me,' she said huskily, taking hold of one of his hands and drawing it determinedly to her thigh. 'Oh, yes, touch me!' She shifted so that his hand moved against her leg. 'You want to—you do want do, don't you?'

Ben closed his eyes, but only briefly. The tantalising caress of her soft skin was too tempting. 'Yes, I want to touch you,' he admitted roughly, acknowledging his surrender. He was already aroused from the shock he had suffered when he had thought she was drowning. Now, intoxicated by the look and the smell and the feel of her, he had no resistance, and he cupped one hand behind her neck and pulled her closer. Then, parting her lips with a probing thumb, he covered her mouth with his.

Her lips opened wide to the hungry penetration of his tongue, sharing its invasion and making tentative invasions of her own. Her senses swam beneath that wet, urgent possession, and a delicious warmth spread through her body, completely banishing any feeling of cold she had felt when she had first come out of the water.

Then, keeping his mouth on hers, he propelled her backwards, and she felt the prickling coolness of the grass against her spine. It was amazingly erotic to feel each individual blade caressing her limbs, stroking the cleft of her bottom, probing each intimate hollow. Her whole body seemed sensitised to every new experience, and when her fingers slid into the silky dampness of his hair she felt an overwhelming sense of exhilaration.

She moaned when his mouth moved from hers, and she dug her nails into his scalp in protest. But then her fingers flexed convulsively when his lips trailed a path of heat down her neck and across her throat. And with sensual mastery he brought one hand up to cup her breast, squeezing the nipple between his thumb and forefinger before taking the engorged peak into his mouth.

She groaned, her hands seeking his hair again, and gripping tightly. She had never dreamed anything could feel so good, or so amazing. When he lifted his head, she badly wanted to beg him to go on, but then he moved to her other breast, and his suckling mouth became a sensual abrasion.

And there was more, much more. After returning to her mouth, to taste again the fevered urgency of her lips, he sought the downy hollow of her stomach, laving her palpitating navel with his tongue. A moist warmth was enveloping every part of her, and she shifted beneath his caress, desperate to sustain these unfamiliar feelings.

But then, to her dismay, he shifted position yet again. In some confusion, he felt him part her legs and touch the sensitive flesh between. The feelings this evoked were infinitely more disturbing, and she shuddered beneath his hands in a helpless state of abandon.

'Oh, please—' she breathed, dry-mouthed, and with a sensual sigh Ben's mouth slid reluctantly back to hers.

'What's the matter?' he chided, the taste of her on his lips. 'Didn't you like it?'

Cass found she was panting now, but she managed to shake her head. 'You know I did,' she whispered unsteadily. 'Perhaps—perhaps too much.'

'Not too much,' he corrected her huskily, his raw male scent filling her nostrils. Then, as his legs tangled sensuously with hers, she discovered he was as naked as she was.

She wanted to touch him, too, and as his mouth grew even more demanding she spread her fingers against the sleek brown flesh of his hips. The tight mound of his buttocks rose beneath her hands as she allowed them to move lower. And as she caressed him he shuddered beneath her touch, betraying his own taut arousal.

'Don't,' he muttered at last, when her explorations brought her to the throbbing muscle between his legs, and she protested.

'Why?'

'Because I want you,' he told her harshly. 'I want to come inside you. Not—' he groaned, 'not in your hands.'

Cass caught her breath, and with barely controlled patience Ben moved between her legs. 'I love you,' he said against her lips as the blunt strength of his manhood nudged the moist tangle of ash-blonde curls. Then, ignoring the instinctive resistance that four years of suffering Roger's insensitive handling had left her with, he entered her, slowly but insistently, penetrating deep into the heart of her being.

He seemed so big at first, so powerful, and she was half afraid her muscles would not expand enough to accommodate him. She almost panicked when it seemed she was not big enough; but Ben had no such hesitation. 'Relax,' he whispered softly against her ear, and then she was filled with a sense of completeness she had never known before.

He was still for a few moments, allowing her to get used to the feel of him inside her, but eventually with infinite tenderness he began to move. She knew he was trying to be patient, which couldn't be easy for him, and she was half inclined to tell him that he needn't be so considerate. But it was difficult to put into words the fact that if some women did get satisfaction from the sexual act she was not one of them. Of course, being with Ben had already been so much more exciting then being with Roger, but ultimately the end was bound to be the same. She was incapable of enjoying sex, with anybody; and she could only hope that when the time came she could fake her own reaction. With a bit of luck, Ben would be too overcome with his own climax to notice, but afterwards she would have to tell him the truth...

Her anxious soul-searching was stilled by the realisation that she couldn't concentrate on practical matters at this moment. The sensual feel of Ben's body as it seemed to pull away from her, only to plunge even more deeply into the contracting muscles of her sheath, was having the most disturbing effect. She found herself lifting her body from the ground to meet his, and when he pushed her down again to the turf, she let out an ecstatic cry. It felt so good to have him deep inside her, but she wanted him deeper still, and almost of their own volition her legs wound around his back to facilitate that ability.

'Good?' he murmured, looking down at her, and she moved her head in a jerky gesture of assent.

'Just go on,' she groaned, digging her fingers into his shoulders, and with a smile of satisfaction he complied.

His hands cupped her buttocks, lifting her even more firmly against him, and her whole being seemed intent on him, and only him. She wanted to wind herself about him, she wanted him to go on and on making this amazing love to her, and where once she had been cold now her body was drenched with fire.

Ben was sweating, too. Her fingers wiped rivulets of moisture from his forehead and smeared them over her own body. The slick wetness of their skin was fusing them together, and her actions were purely instinctive and mindlessly sexual.

She didn't think she could go on enduring such excitement. Her heart was pounding in her chest, leaping against the wall of her ribs, as if it was determined to break free. Her whole being seemed poised on the brink of some ultimate new discovery, and she was aching for a fulfilment that only Ben could give her.

And when it happened she could hardly believe it. The splintering waves of pleasure that had been sweeping her up, and up, suddenly reached their pinnacle, and the moment was so unique that she almost lost consciousness. But she was aware of Ben calling her name, and of his own simultaneous release, which caused a burning flood of warmth inside her. And then, as he collapsed upon her, the wave let her go, and she drifted back to earth in a blissful state of lethargy...

It seemed hours later that she opened her eyes to find Ben had rolled on to his side, and was lying, looking at her. But it could only have been a few minutes. The heaviness of her lids seemed to indicate a shorter spell of rest, and she closed her eyes again abruptly, not wanting to lose the delicious feeling of languor that was gripping her.

'Hey,' he said, using a blade of grass to tickle her chin, 'do you have any idea what time it is?'

Cass groaned. 'Does it matter?'

'I think so.' Ben propped himself up on his elbow, drawing up one leg to support his other arm. 'By my reckoning, it's going to be the early hours of the morning before we get back to Calvado. I just hope my mother's gone to bed. I don't think I could take facing her tonight.'

Cass sighed, and opened her eyes. 'Don't worry,' she said, lifting a hand to stroke his cheek. 'I'll be with you.'

Ben caught his lower lip between his teeth, looking at her with something almost akin to pity, and then he slowly shook his head. 'No, you won't.'

'What do you mean?' She blinked. 'Of course I will. Now that I know we're not related, do you think I'm going to leave you?' She caught her breath. 'Don't be silly. I don't care what Daddy says now.'

'But I do.' Removing her hand from his cheek, Ben got abruptly to his feet. 'You'd better get dressed. I want to get moving.'

Cass swallowed the lump which seemed to have developed in her throat and sat up. 'What do you mean?' she asked, looking up at him. 'Why should you care what Daddy thinks? He can't hurt you.'

'No. He can't hurt me,' Ben agreed, picking up his jeans and beginning to turn the legs the right way out. In his haste to get to Cass, he had simply torn them off, and she watched him put the trousers to rights with open-mouthed confusion.

'Ben,' she exclaimed after a moment, as he stepped into the jeans and zipped them up. 'Ben, please, we have to talk. Stop behaving as if you regret what just happened. I don't regret it. It was the most marvellous experience of my life!'

'I know.' Ben paused and looked down at her; and then, as if the sight of her sitting there like some woodland naiad penetrated the wall he was trying to erect between them, and he gave a groan of desperation. 'Cass,' he muttered, throwing aside his shirt and squatting down beside her, 'don't look at me like that. I need you to try and understand.'

Cass help up her head. 'What is there to understand?'

She lifted her slim shoulders. 'That you're like Daddy, even if you're not his son? That what just happened was just sex? That it didn't mean the same to you as it did to me?'

'Don't be foolish!' A muscle was jerking in Ben's cheek, and the hand resting on his thigh clenched into a fist. And then, as if the words were torn from him, he said, 'What happened just now was—inevitable. I've wanted you for so long...' He shook his head. 'There have been no other women. Not since that summer you were eighteen, at least. The idea was abhorrent to me. I've buried myself in my work, in my teaching, in this book I'm having such trouble right now in writing. Until you came, begging my help, I'd almost succeeded in convincing myself that I didn't need anyone else. But that night, at the apartment, I realised how wrong I had been.'

'Then stop talking as if this is all we're ever going to have,' Cass whispered, stretching out her hand and running her nail down the zip of his jeans. 'We don't have to worry about anyone, any more. I just wonder why you took so long to tell me. You must have known how I felt all along.'

'No!' Expelling a taut breath, Ben forced her hand away from the stirring reaction of his body. 'You still don't understand, do you? What *Nonna* told you—what she told me, when I was about the same age—is not our secret to tell.'

Cass blinked. 'But why is it a secret?' she exclaimed. 'It's not as if your mother and my father are still married!'

'No.' Ben conceded the point, but he got to his feet again as he did so, and the awful sense of apprehension flooded over her again.

'Oh, please—' she cried, gazing up at him. 'What are you saying? That Daddy doesn't know you're not his son?

Well, what does it matter? It's not as if you're hoping to inherit the company!' Her eyes widened in dismay. 'Or—are you?'

Ben's face contorted. 'If that's what you want to believe.'

'It's not what I want to believe.' Cass scrambled to her feet now. 'I'm only trying to make some sense of what you're saying. Ben, stop behaving as if we're enemies. I love you! Doesn't that mean anything any more?'

'Oh, Cass!' His response to her was unmistakable, but instead of taking her in his arms he bent and picked up her clothes and pushed them at her. 'Get dressed,' he said flatly. 'I can't think sensibly with you in that state.'

'Perhaps I don't want you to think sensibly,' she muttered tearfully. But she took the dress and panties, and silently put them on, squeezing the ends of her hair before picking up her sandals. 'Satisfied?'

Ben avoided that question, concentrating on the task of putting on his own shoes. Then he gestured that they should return the way they had come, and scuffing her toes in the grass Cass accompanied him obediently back to the car.

But once inside the Porsche Ben didn't immediately start the engine. 'Look,' he said heavily, 'I don't know how to say this, but when I brought you here, I wanted this to happen.'

'You did?' Cass tried not to be too optimistic. Something told her that whatever Ben was going to say, ultimately it would not be good. But she had to listen.

'Yes.' He laid his hands on the wheel, flexing his fingers as he obviously struggled to find the right words. 'Call me selfish, if you like, but I'd come back to Calvado because I couldn't stay away from you. Lord,' he thrust his fingers into his hair, 'you have no idea how many sleepless nights you've cost me.'

'Ben...'

She touched his sleeve, but he shook her off. 'No,' he said. 'You've got to hear me out. I need to tell you.'

'That you wanted me,' she asked softly. 'I'm glad. Is that why you've spent so much time with Carlo, and your mother?'

'What do you think?' Ben was ironic. 'The day I found you on the beach—alone—it was pure frustration that made me yell at you. Oh, I don't approve of you swimming there alone. It could be dangerous. But, seeing you half naked, wanting to touch you and not having the right to do so, nearly drove me insane.'

Cass expelled an unsteady breath. 'I thought you were mad at me. When I asked if you were like Daddy, you almost flipped.'

'Yes. Well, I did have some justification,' he responded drily. 'It was bad enough knowing the truth and not being able to tell you, without you throwing Guido's sexual exploits in my face.'

'Then, why—'

'Not yet.' He bent his head. 'This morning when you came down to breakfast and accused me of avoiding you, I couldn't take it any more. I decided I would take you to Verrazzino, and to hell with the consequences.'

'You wanted your grandmother to tell me?'

'Hell, no!' He groaned. 'I never thought she'd tell you, not Guido Scorcese's daughter. No.' He shook his head. 'I was going to do the telling. I just wanted *Nonna* to back me up.'

'And?' Cass had difficulty in articulating the word.

'And when I got there, I found I couldn't do it,' he said simply.

'Why—why not?'

'Why do you think?' He spoke wearily now. 'Because I realised I couldn't do that to my mother. I've kept her secret for more than fifteen years, and much as I wanted to be free of all the lies and deceit, I knew there was no way I could betray her trust.'

Cass trembled. 'And that was why you were so tense after we reached your grandmother's house?'

Ben grimaced. 'It was that obvious, hmm?'

'Well—to me,' she murmured honestly.

'So, how did *Nonna* come to tell you?' he asked suddenly. 'She's not usually so indiscreet with strangers.'

'Oh...' Cass bent her head. 'There was a photograph on the dresser. I thought it was you.'

'And because of that—'

'She guessed how I felt about you,' exclaimed Cass with harsh emotion. 'She asked if I loved you, and—and I didn't deny it. I suppose she put two and two together.'

Ben's lips twisted. 'She's a shrewd old lady.'

'Yes.' Cass took a steadying breath, and lifted her head. 'So—what now?'

'Now?' His fingers curled about the wheel. 'Now comes the hardest part.' He stared straight ahead. 'We go on as before.'

'No!' Her cry was anguished.

'We must.'

'But, why? Why?' Cass was desperate now. 'If, as you say, you don't care whether Daddy leaves you a part of the company or not, what have you to lose?'

'Me?'

'Well—Sophia, then! As I see it—'

His hand on her shoulder silenced her headstrong outburst, and she closed her eyes against the ache of longing his lean fingers aroused in her still. 'Listen to me,' he said harshly. 'You know my mother. You know what a proud woman she is. Can you imagine what this would do to her? If Guido was to find out that I was not his son, don't you realise how he would feel?'

Cass moved her head in a negative gesture. 'He—he would be—surprised—'

'*Surprised?*' Ben was scathing. 'He wouldn't be *surprised*! He'd be bloody furious! For heaven's sake, the man's been supporting Sophia for the past thirty-seven years!'

'I know—'

'Then you also know that he wouldn't have provided her with the Villa Andrea without believing he was doing it for me as well, for his *son!*'

'Oh, Ben!'

'Now, do you begin to understand?' he demanded, and suddenly realising his fingers were digging into her soft flesh he withdrew them. 'I'm sorry.'

Cass felt sick. 'You can't mean this.'

'I'm afraid I do.' Ben's face was grim when she looked at him. 'Believe me, if there was anything that could be done, I'd have done it.' His mouth took on a bitter slant. 'Once—just once, I came close to destroying everything.' He paused. 'Do you remember? When I came to London to see you?'

Cass was so distraught, she could hardly think straight. 'To see me?' she echoed. She didn't remember him ever coming to London just to see her.

'Yes.' Ben was patient. 'Four years ago?' he prompted.

'Four years ago?' Cass's brows drew together perplexedly. 'But—but that was when—'

'—when we'd acknowledged what was between us, I know,' said Ben flatly. 'Or, at least, I thought we had.'

'What do you mean?' She was confused. 'You—you sent me away!'

Ben groaned. 'You must know how hard that was now.'

Cass blinked. 'But—but you were horrible! You called me all sorts of names! You said I was spoilt—and self-ish—'

'And I meant it,' he declared grimly. 'How do you think I felt when I got to London and the first thing your mother told me was that you were engaged to Roger Fielding?'

Cass caught her breath. 'Mummy told you that?'

'It was true, wasn't it?'

'Oh…' Cass made a defeated little gesture. 'In a manner of speaking, I suppose.'

'What do you mean?' Ben was confused now. 'Either you were, or you weren't.'

Cass shook her head. 'It wasn't that simple.' She sighed, realising she had to explain, in however bad a light it painted her. 'After—after I got back from Italy, I flew out to Bermuda. You know Daddy has the villa near Hamilton? Well, he and Mummy were spending the summer there, and—and I needed them.'

'Go on.'

'So, Roger was there, too. But you know that, don't you? Well, I was pretty wild after what had happened. In any event, I got drunk, at a party, and—and we had sex.'

'Oh, Cass!'

Ben's compassion almost overwhelmed her, but she forced herself to go on. 'Anyway, because of that, Roger proposed. And—and I accepted. I realise now, it was mainly to get back at you, and I'm not proud of it, but I did it anyway.'

'Oh, hell!' Ben rested his elbows on the wheel, and propped his head in his hands.

'I knew—I knew as soon as I got back to England that I'd made a mistake, and when Mrs Auden came to tell me you were with Mummy, I thought you had come to tell me you'd forgiven me.'

'Forgiven you?' Ben groaned. 'Dear heaven, I came to tell you the truth. But when your mother—'

'Don't say it!' Cass put trembling hands over her ears. 'Don't say any more. I can't bear it.'

'Ah, Cass!'

At last her bitter despair got through to him and, giving in to emotions stronger than himself, he pulled her into his arms. She pressed herself against him urgently, her arms so tight around his neck that he could scarcely move at all.

'Hey,' he said, as her shaking body revealed that she was sobbing. 'Don't, *cara*. Please, don't.'

'Are—are you going to send me away again?' she faltered, resisting his efforts to wipe away her tears with his thumb, and he heaved a heavy sigh.

'I have to.'

'But—but you were going to tell the truth four years ago,' she protested, and he at last succeeded in drawing back.

'Was I?' he asked, and she caught her breath. 'Who knows? I might have chickened out at the last minute, as I did today.'

'Ben…'

'No, I mean it.' He was ironic. 'It's easy now for me to say what I *intended* to do. But, if I'm honest—' He shrugged. 'Who knows?'

Cass drew back in her seat. She felt utterly exhausted. And defeated. No way was Ben going to betray his mother now. Sophia had won. Again! She *always* won.

'What will you do?' Ben asked at last, as if the question

had been torn out of him, and Cass managed an indifferent shrug.

'I don't know.' She hesitated. 'I shall go back to London, of course.'

'When?'

'Probably tomorrow.'

'No!'

'Yes.' Now it was her turn to be adamant. 'I can't stay here, Ben. Not now.'

'Oh, *hell*!'

With a violent movement, he flicked the ignition, and when the engine fired he thrust it savagely into gear. The tyres spun as they cleared the damp grass, but then they were on the road, and the car took command. With a smooth efficiency that owed little to Ben's clenched hands on the wheel, it ate up the miles between Verrazzino and Calvado, and at least one of its occupants had the unworthy hope that they might not make it…

CHAPTER TWELVE

'BUT you can't stay here!'

Diana Scorcese's voice mirrored her impatience. She looked round the decidedly untidy living-room with scornful eyes, seeing nothing of merit in the comfortably worn cushions of the sofa, or in the tightly packed shelves of books that lined the walls. To her eyes, Maggie's whole apartment was an abomination, and she couldn't imagine how any daughter of hers could consider living in such surroundings.

Trying another tack, she gave Cass one of her most appealing looks, and ruefully shook her head. 'Darling, you know what Daddy's going to say when he discovers where you are. It was bad enough you flying off to Italy without telling a soul where you'd gone. But how d'you think he's going to feel if he finds you're living in this place? If you insist on not going back to the house in Knightsbridge, at least have the decency to come home.'

'No.' Cass coiled one leg beneath her, and sank down into a corner of the sofa. 'But don't worry. This is only a temporary squat. As soon as I can find somewhere more suitable, I'll move out. Maggie is leaving for the States in less than a week, and she says I can crash here until she gets back.'

Diana's lips curled at her daughter's vocabulary, but she refrained from making the automatic retort that Cass had expected. Instead, she seated herself with some reluctance on the edge of the chair opposite and, crossing one silk-clad leg over the other, she tried once again to be reasonable.

'But what about Roger?' she exclaimed, and seeing Cass's face close up she leant forward and gripped her daughter's arm. 'Darling, we have to talk about it. Sooner or later, he's bound to find out you're back in London. Surely the most sensible course would be to see him? Your father says he's in quite a state. I'm sure he regrets what happened, as we all do.'

Cass held up her head. 'No, Mummy.'

'But, Cass—'

'Mummy, when I agreed to see you, you promised you'd tell nobody where I was.'

'And I haven't.' Diana sighed. 'But that doesn't mean I approve of you hiding out here like a criminal. Heaven knows, no one likes to find their husband is being unfaithful to them, but it's not the end of the world!' She moved her shoulders impatiently. 'Men are not like women, Cass. They need their little—adventures! Roger doesn't love this woman he's been sleeping with. He loves you. If you agreed to take him back— '

'No, Mummy!' Cass was adamant. 'I want a divorce, and—and I intend to get one.'

'Oh, my goodness!' Biting back a coarser expletive, Diana got abruptly to her feet, pacing to the window and back again with unconcealed frustration. 'Your father will never agree to it.'

'He doesn't have to,' retorted Cass tightly, hoping she sounded more confident than she felt. 'Mummy, this isn't the first time Roger's done something like this. You know what happened a couple of years ago. But Daddy intervened, and—'

'And he would intervene again,' exclaimed Diana, but Cass shook her head.

'No.'

'Why not?' Diana was eager. 'Darling, this time you can be sure Roger wouldn't get away unscathed. I'd see to that.'

'No.'

'Oh, Cass!' Diana expelled her breath on a gasp. 'This is ridiculous! You're not giving him a chance. At least see him, talk to him.'

'I have seen him.'

'I know.' Diana's lips pulled in. 'At Ben's apartment.'

'Yes.'

'But how could you talk then? With—with Sophia's son as an unwelcome onlooker!'

'He wasn't.' Cass looked up at her mother, frowning. 'Is that what Roger told you?'

'Maybe.' Diana was vague now. 'I think Ben's name was mentioned, but I could be wrong.'

Cass looked sceptical. 'What you mean is, Roger lied to you, just as he's lied to me,' she retorted. 'As a matter of fact, Ben did come back while Roger was there. Just in time to throw him out!'

Diana's expression hardened. 'I knew it.' She came back to where Cass was sitting and glared down at her. 'I knew that man had had some part in your decision. It's he who's put you up to this, isn't it? He's been nothing but trouble as long as I've known him.'

Cass gave her mother a cool stare. 'I thought you liked him.'

'Me?' Diana made a disparaging gesture, but she didn't meet her daughter's eyes. 'Just because I've always been civil to him, it doesn't mean I actually *like* the man. Good heavens, Cass, I'm friendly with lots of people. But you must know as well as anyone, that expediency often plays the greater part.'

Cass tilted her head. 'And why was it expedient to be friendly with Ben?'

'Oh…' Diana was on the spot, and she obviously didn't like it. 'Well, he is your father's son, isn't he? Can you imagine how *he* would react if I treated Ben as a pariah? No, obviously I've always welcomed him into our house. But I've never cared for your involvement with him, and I—I resent very much the fact that you turned to him when you should have turned to us.'

Having succeeded in diverting the course of the conversation, Diana returned to the window again, dabbing her upper lip with a lace-trimmed handkerchief. And, watching her, Cass knew a weary sense of resignation. No matter how long she avoided seeing either Roger or her father, sooner or later she was going to have to face both of them. Scoring points off her mother was not going to get her anywhere. Diana was comparatively easy to defeat. Guido Scorcese was most definitely not.

'All right,' she said at last, getting to her feet, shaking the creases out of the baggy white trousers she was wearing, and Diana turned.

''All right—what?'' she enquired cautiously, and Cass pushed her hands into her pockets.

'All right, I'll see Daddy,' she declared, her nails digging painfully into her palms. 'But not here. I'll come to the house. Would tonight be too soon, or has he got an engagement?'

Diana swallowed. 'Oh—well, we are supposed to be dining with the Conways,' she murmured, 'but I suppose I could put them off.'

'Good.' Cass endeavoured to sustain her air of indifference. 'About seven o'clock, then? Would that be all right?'

'Fine. Fine.' Diana came towards her daughter eagerly

now, obviously much relieved at this unexpected concession. 'Until tonight, then, darling,' she murmured, kissing the air beside Cass's cheek. 'Oh—and you will wear something a little more—conservative, won't you? You know how your father hates you to dress like that.'

With the door closed behind Diana, Cass leaned weakly back against it. She was trembling, she found, and it annoyed her that speaking to her mother should have proved such an ordeal. However was she going to cope with her father that evening? Perhaps she should have made it tomorrow, or the day after. But the idea of delaying the inevitable was equally as unattractive, and the sooner she got it over with, the better.

Moving away from the door, she ran unsteady hands up the sides of her neck to cup her cheeks. Then, with a feeling of utter weariness, she flopped down on the sofa again.

She knew she ought to be contemplating what she was going to say to her father that evening, but she didn't have the strength. Besides, everything she did nowadays had a curious sense of unreality to it, and sometimes she wanted to pinch herself to make sure she wasn't dreaming.

But it was no dream. She was here, in this small apartment in London, owned by Maggie Auden, the daughter of Mrs Auden, who had been her parents' housekeeper for years. She and Maggie had been friends, ever since they were children, even if that friendship had been sometimes strained by Diana's obvious disapproval. Of a similar age—Maggie was actually two years older than Cass—the two girls had shared many confidences over the years. And Mrs Auden had never objected when her employer's daughter had sought company, and sometimes comfort, in the kitchen at Eaton Chare. Of course, after Maggie went away to university, and Cass got married, their friendship had begun to drift. Their lives were so divergent, and Cass had never been able to tell anyone what a disaster her life with Roger had become. She had been too ashamed.

But when she arrived back in London a week ago pride was no longer a problem. Sick and hopeless, desperate for consolation, she hadn't hesitated before phoning Maggie, and once again her friend had been there for her.

Naturally, she had not been able to confide everything to Maggie. So far as the other girl was concerned, she had gone to Italy to give herself time to think about her relationship with Roger—which was true—and now she was back in London again, still undecided about her future.

To Maggie, there was no contest. If Roger had been unfaithful, Cass had every right to want a divorce. So far as she was concerned, she and her mother had never cared for Roger Fielding, and they had both been surprised at the precipitation with which Cass had married him. After all, she had hardly known him before she went to Bermuda, and having sex with someone was hardly a reason for matrimony these days.

Cass had known she was right but, without involving Ben, she couldn't explain her reasons for behaving so recklessly. But she did take the blame for what had happened, and when Maggie pointed out that Roger must have been pretty desperate to propose in those circumstances, she said that because she had been a virgin he had obviously felt compelled to do so.

Maggie had pulled a wry face at this, but she had kept her own counsel, and during the past week Cass had known a brief respite from emotional tension. Her problems hadn't gone away; they were still as acute as ever. But living with Maggie was so far removed from her normal existence that she was able to practice a kind of self-hypnosis, and numb herself to everything else.

At least, during the day that was so. Night-time was another matter. Oh, she slept. Some sleeping tablets Maggie had very reluctantly got her from the chemist had seen to that. But her sleep was punctuated with violent dreams, and she always awakened in the early hours of the morning, weak, the sheets soaked with sweat, and the pillow tear-stained.

And that was when the painful memories would not be denied. And they were painful, excruciatingly so. Not least, the scene that had erupted when they had got back from Verrazzino, and found Ben's mother waiting for them...

It was getting light as they drove down the twisting track to the villa. The sky was pale yellow, and streaked with cotton-wool clouds that would melt away as soon as the sun gained any heat. There was moisture on the grass, and the delicious smell of mimosa, mingling with the pine scent that coated the wooded hillside. It was so beautiful, Cass wanted to weep. But crying was an indulgence she couldn't afford right now.

'Are you all right?'

They were the first words Ben had said to her for hours, and she turned her head to look at him. 'Are you?'

'No.' His hands tightened on the wheel. 'Are you sure you won't think again?'

'About staying?' Cass's lips twisted. 'I don't think so.'

'But why?' His question was tormented. 'Cass, this may be the only time we'll have together. Don't throw it away!'

'I have to.' She turned back to the view. 'You expect too much, Ben. I'm not that good an actress. Your—your mother wouldn't be deceived for a minute. Oh, lord!' She broke off abruptly. 'There she is!'

'Oh, no!'

Ben's reaction was weary, and Cass knew an over-whelming need to comfort him. But she couldn't. Apart from anything else, he wouldn't want her to. Not with Sophia waiting for them, and able to see every response. But it did seem the final ignominy, and Cass wondered what on earth she hoped to achieve.

Sophia was waiting in the garden, a woollen cardigan about her shoulders, protecting her arms from the chill of the dawning day. Cass, who hadn't even noticed the cool-ness of the air until that point, suddenly felt shivery. But she guessed it was more a psychological reaction than any real consequence of the cold.

Ben parked the Porsche in its usual place, and then gave Cass one final entreating look. 'Change your mind.'

It was the hardest thing Cass had ever done, but she shook her head. 'I can't.'

'OK.' The muscles of his face clenching into a tight mask, Ben didn't argue with her. He thrust open his door and got out. 'Hello, *Mamma!*' He greeted his mother in Italian. 'You're an early riser. It's barely five a.m.'

Sophia didn't immediately answer him. Instead, she strode towards him, and while Cass watched with unbe-lieving horror she delivered a stunning blow to his cheek. '*Bastardo!*' she choked, the stream of words that followed it, too unspeakable to be repeated. 'Where have you been? What have you been doing?' Her eyes darted back to the car, as Cass was struggling to get out. 'How dare you take her with you. I will never forgive you. *Never!*'

Ben said nothing. He just stood there, facing his mother, rubbing his reddening cheek with one hand. He was wearing a curiously remote expression, as if his mother's words, and the blow she had delivered, meant nothing to him. He seemed indifferent to her questions, or her vituperation, and his attitude disturbed Cass as she came to stand beside him.

'It was my fault,' she said, steeling herself to face his mother, and Sophia looked at her contemptuously.

'I can believe it.'

'It was.' Cass cast Ben a worried look, and when he didn't respond she was forced to go on. 'It was late when we left Verrazzino, and then I insisted on going swimming.'

'*Swimming?*'

Sophia almost screamed the word, and as if the shrillness of her voice had at last got through to him Ben intervened. 'Don't bother to explain yourself, Cass,' he said flatly. 'Whatever you say, she won't believe you. Go on, go to bed. This isn't going to resolve anything, and you must be exhausted.'

'You're tired, too...' began Cass unsteadily, but his hand in the small of her back was pushing her towards the villa.

'Go to bed,' he advised harshly, ignoring Sophia's bitter protest. 'I can handle this. Please, go! Don't say anything more.'

Cass had wanted to stay with him. She had wanted to tell Sophia exactly what had happened, and who she blamed for this whole sordid mess. But, of course, she didn't. Ben looked so weary, so haggard, so utterly unlike his normal self, that she felt compelled to obey him. But that didn't block her ears to the terrible row that followed, or give her any respite from the raw anguish of her thoughts.

However, after more than an hour, when an ominous silence had fallen on the villa, she tiptoed down the stairs and found Ben alone in the *salone*, and she discovered it was too late also to have a change of heart. When she crossed the floor to his side, her bare feet making little sound on the tiled floor, he refused point-blank to let her stay on at the villa.

'You were right,' he said, his voice totally devoid of emotion. 'You can't stay here. I was crazy ever to suggest it. Go back to England, Cass. That's where you belong.'

Her friend came home as Cass was getting ready to go out. Maggie worked as a researcher at a museum in Kensington, and this apartment near Holland Park was close enough for her to walk to work. She looked surprised when she saw the other girl had washed her silky hair and put on the suede suit she had worn to travel in. Since Cass had taken up residence at the apartment, she'd dressed in nothing but jeans or casual trousers and sloppy T-shirts, and she had certainly not worn lipstick or a delicate green eyeliner.

'You phoned your mother, then?' Maggie remarked, tossing her shoulder-bag on to a chair, and Cass nodded.

'Yes. She came round this afternoon. I—er—I've agreed to go and see Daddy. Do you think I'm doing the right thing?'

Maggie grimaced. She was a small girl, plumper than Cass, with a mass of curly chestnut-coloured hair. At this time of the year, her face was covered with freckles, and as she seldom wore make-up she almost never looked her age.

'I suppose you have to,' she said at last. 'I know Mum said Mr Scorcese has been very worried about you.'

'Yes.' Cass was still doubtful. 'I told Mummy it was you who suggested I make the call.'

Maggie pulled a face. 'I bet that endeared me to her,'

she said, pulling a pack of beefburgers out of a plastic carrier with 'Marks & Spencer' emblazoned on the side. She smiled. 'You're not worried about seeing him, are you? He is your father, after all. And I'm sure he really loves you.'

'Hmm.' Cass sighed. 'I wish you could come with me.'

'I don't think that would be wise.' Maggie was sympathetic. 'Just—tell them how you feel. They can't make you stay with Roger. Tell them how he threatened you in Ben's apartment. I bet you didn't tell your mother that.'

'No, I didn't.' Cass shook her head. 'It sounds so—so melodramatic, somehow. What if they don't believe me? What if Roger's already given them his version? Oh, Maggie, I wish—I wish—'

'—Ben was here,' finished her friend shrewdly. Then, colouring, she looked away. 'I'd better put these under the grill,' she added, indicating the burgers. 'I don't suppose you want any supper, do you? You'll probably be having something infinitely more sophisticated.'

Cass didn't contradict her, even though food was the farthest thing from her thoughts at this moment. What did Maggie mean? What must her friend be thinking? If only she could tell her the truth, how much simpler life would be...

CHAPTER THIRTEEN

CASS had left her keys at the house in Knightsbridge when she'd first left England, so Mrs Auden had to let her in when she arrived at Eaton Chare. 'Why, Cass!' she exclaimed warmly, giving the girl a swift hug after closing the door behind her. 'It's so good to see you again. It must be all of six weeks. We've all been so worried about you.'

'Have you?' Cass managed a faint smile. 'Well, Maggie's taken good care of me.'

Mrs Auden shook her head. 'You should have come home,' she said reprovingly.

Home? Cass wondered what the housekeeper would say if she told her she didn't have a home. Not really. She couldn't go back to the house in Knightsbridge, and she had the feeling that Diana, at least, would not welcome her back here.

'Anyway, your mother's in the library,' said Mrs Auden now, and Cass wondered if she only imagined the rather anxious expression that crossed the housekeeper's face as she urged her towards the stairs. 'Er—come and see me before you go.'

The first-floor library at Eaton Chare served the dual purpose of providing Guido Scorcese with a comfortable room where he could work, and a pleasant space where he could entertain his business colleagues. However, on other occasions, like now, for instance, it could be used as a place to gather for drinks before dinner, and when Cass opened the door she had no suspicion that her mother

186

might not be alone. She was early, and Mrs Auden's announcement that her mother was waiting for her had made her think that her father wasn't yet home. But the sight of Roger Fielding, lounging in one of the buttoned leather armchairs that flanked her father's desk, sent her backing out of the room, and only her mother's impatient summons prevented her from rushing out of the house.

'Cass, for goodness' sake!' Her mother, who had been standing unobserved beside the long windows that overlooked the square, came quickly after her, catching Cass's arm before she started down the stairs again. 'Cass, please! I will not have this kind of behaviour in my house! Now, Roger has come here at my invitation, to speak to you. At least have the decency to hear what he has to say. He is your husband, after all. He does have some rights.'

Cass's nostrils flared. 'Mummy, you tricked me—'

'I didn't trick you.' Diana's voice was low and indignant. 'Your father will be here shortly. I just thought it might be a good idea if you and Roger had a chance to talk before Guido arrives. This is your problem, you know. Not your father's.'

Cass gazed at her mother with weary eyes. 'Do you think I don't know that?'

'Very well, then.'

'Oh, all right, Mummy.' Cass gave in. 'But I don't want to see Roger alone. I'd like you to stay with me.'

'Oh, really, Cass—' Diana was beginning irritably, when Roger himself came out of the library.

'Please, Cass,' he said, his tone vastly different from that which he had used in Ben's apartment. 'I've been almost out of my mind with worry. You don't know what it's been like, knowing you've been ill, and not being allowed to see you. You're my wife, for heaven's sake!' He exchanged a quick look with Diana, and then went on,

'Your mother knows how I feel. She's been a real brick. That's why she arranged this meeting. She's prepared to give me another chance.'

Cass held up her head. 'Well, I'm not.'

'I don't accept that.'

'I don't care with you accept.'

'Oh, for heaven's sake,' Diana protested, 'at least give him a chance to tell you how he feels!' She paused. 'Look, I've got to go and speak to Mrs Auden about supper. You two have a chat, and when I get back—'

'Mummy—'

'Stop being childish, Cassandra.' Diana was losing her temper and it showed. 'I will not allow you to make a fool of me like this. I insist that you speak to Roger. If you refuse, I shall tell your father, and Roger, where you're staying, and they will take it from there.'

Cass knew she was beaten. If Roger or her father found out where she was staying, her brief spell of freedom would be over. Besides, she couldn't do that to Maggie. It wasn't fair to her to be forced into the middle of what was, essentially, a family argument.

The library was delightfully cool after the somewhat muggy warmth of the evening outside. Its booklined walls retained heat in winter, and repelled it in summer. Consequently, the temperature was invariably pleasant.

Not so the atmosphere, however. Particularly this evening. Allowing Roger to close the door behind them, Cass felt a distinct sense of chill, and she guessed that Roger's reasonable manner had been for Diana's ears alone.

'So,' he said, walking round her as she stood uneasily in the middle of the floor, 'you decided to come back.'

Cass took a breath. 'I'm here, aren't I?'

'But you're not living at home.'

'If you mean the house in Knightsbridge, I don't consider that my home any more,' replied Cass steadily.

'I see.' Roger halted in front of her. 'So you're determined to go through with it, then?'

'Leaving you, you mean? Yes.'

'Even if it means losing your father, too?'

Cass trembled. 'I won't lose my father.'

'No?' Roger's lips twisted.

'No.'

'Not even if I tell him why you're doing this?'

Cass swallowed. 'I intend to tell him myself.'

'Do you?' Roger's expression was almost admiring. 'Well, I'll certainly be interested to hear how he reacts to the fact that *his* son and *his* daughter are more than just good friends.'

Cass went pale. 'What do you mean?'

'Do I have to draw you a picture?' Roger returned to the chair he had been occupying earlier and crossed his legs. Evidently, he had delivered his bombshell now, and was quite prepared to enjoy her consternation. 'I may be gullible, Cass, but I'm not a fool. I saw the way Ben looked at you when he found me at the apartment, and it wasn't at all the way a man looks at his kid sister. If he could have killed me and got away with it, he would have done it.'

'Don't be ridiculous!'

It was all Cass could think of to say at that moment, but Roger knew he had struck a raw nerve, and he capitalised on it.

'It's not ridiculous. It's sick!' he retorted coldly, his eyes never leaving her revealing features. The colour, which had previously drained away, was now returning to stain her cheeks a vivid scarlet. 'How long has this been going on, I wonder? How many other trips have you made to Florence without my being aware of them?'

'None! That is…' Cass cast about for a means to defend herself, desperate now for some way to allay his suspicions. 'You can't honestly believe there's any truth in what you're saying. I—I've known Ben since I was a child.'

'Which makes it all the more reprehensible,' retorted Roger harshly. 'Oh, yes, your father is not going to enjoy this story. It explains everything. Not least the fact why *I* was forced to go elsewhere for—'

'Roger, you can't!' The cry was torn from her. 'You couldn't tell Daddy something like that. It's not true.'

'It sounds pretty feasible to me,' Roger countered. 'Oh, yes!' He got to his feet abruptly, and paced excitedly about the room. 'You know, you may have done me a favour. This could be exactly the lever I needed.'

Cass felt as if she couldn't possibly take any more, but she had to ask, 'What lever? What are you talking about?'

'This story,' said Roger, halting in front of her again and smiling maliciously. 'What do you think the gutter Press would make of it, hmm? Oh, I can see the headlines now!'

And so could Cass. And they appalled her.

With a feeling of utter degradation, she sank down on to the side of her father's desk. 'So what's your price?' she asked unsteadily. 'What do I have to do to make you give up this—this crazy idea?'

'Not such a crazy idea, or you wouldn't be asking me that,' retorted Roger harshly. But he was obviously considering the alternatives. An expensive scandal, with probably a handsome pay-off; or the obvious advantages of remaining Guido Scorcese's son-in-law and ultimately his successor. It was really no contest. 'We make up,' he decided at last. 'A passionate reunion, and eventually the grandson your father's so eager for.'

Cass felt sick. She couldn't do it, she thought wildly. Not after Ben! But the alternative was too ugly to consider; and although the idea of resuming marital relations with Roger was abhorrent to her she had little doubt that, in time, he would once more seek Valerie Jordan's company.

'Very well,' she said now, but before he could make any comment she had a proviso to add. 'If—if you'll give me a couple of days to—to get used to the idea. After all,' she gathered confidence, 'my mother is hardly likely to believe we've settled our differences in—in fifteen minutes.'

Cass didn't stay for supper. After learning that her father was actually attending a business dinner, and wouldn't be home until much later, she made her excuses and left.

Roger played his part to perfection. His rueful explanation that he and Cass had made some progress, and were going to meet again the following day, completely convinced Diana that she had done the right thing in bringing them together. 'I knew you were exaggerating your differences, darling,' she exclaimed as she saw Cass into a taxi. 'Now, go back to Maggie's and get a good night's sleep. I'll tell Daddy all about it, and he'll probably get in touch with you himself tomorrow.'

Maggie was out, much to Cass's relief, and after giving in to a storm of tears that left her red-eyed and exhausted she made herself a cup of cocoa and went to bed. But not to sleep. She couldn't believe she could feel so tired and not lose consciousness, but she did. When the doorbell rang, she was almost relieved to have to get out of bed and put on her dressing-gown and go and answer it. But she didn't make the mistake of opening the door without first identifying the visitor. After this evening's fiasco, that scene in Florence was very distinct in her mind.

'Who is it?' she called, holding the lapels of the gown close about her. Whoever it was would have to come back tomorrow. She had no intention of admitting anyone in her present state of undress.

'My name is Valerie Jordan,' came the very feminine voice from the other side of the door, and Cass took a sudden backward step. Valerie Jordan? *The* Valerie Jordan? Roger's mistress! It was incredible! What was she doing here? Was Roger with her? No, that was ridiculous. He didn't know where she was. *Or did he?* After tonight, she could hardly trust her mother.

Licking her lips, she took a breath. 'What do you want?'

'I want to speak to—Mrs Fielding,' came the answer. 'Is that Mrs Fielding? Please, can I come in?'

Cass was incredulous. 'You want to come in?' she echoed. 'Is my husband with you?'

'Roger? Of course not.' She sounded as if that suggestion was quite ludicrous. 'Oh, please, Cass—it is Cass, isn't it?—I have to talk to you. Open the door. I promise, I am alone.'

'It's late,' said Cass quickly, leaning back against the door. *Why had the woman come here?*

'It's barely nine o'clock,' returned Valerie Jordan reasonably. 'That's not late.'

It wasn't, but Cass had hardly been aware of the time. 'I don't think we have anything to say to one another, Miss Jordan,' she insisted. 'If you don't go away, I'll—'

'But it's not *Miss* Jordan,' Valerie broke in. 'It's *Mrs*— Mrs *Fielding*, actually. Roger married me six years ago. Two years before he bigamously married you.'

Cass's fingers were all thumbs as she tore open the door, and the woman who was waiting to be admitted permitted herself a small smile at her obvious urgency. 'I thought you might be interested,' she remarked, when Cass stepped back to allow her to enter the living-room. 'So this is where you've been staying. Quite a come-down from Eaton Chare, isn't it?'

'Not in my opinion.' Cass was having the greatest difficulty in containing her patience. Why didn't Valerie explain why she had decided to come here now? What if she had been lying? What if it had just been a ruse to get in here? The thought that she might have been lying turned Cass's legs to jelly.

Oh, lord, she thought, it had to be true!

Although she had seen Valerie before, it had never been at such close quarters, and the other woman's cool, elegant appearance did nothing for Cass's self-esteem. Her dark hair curled becomingly about rounded cheekbones, and her rather voluptuous figure was shown to advantage in a close-fitting linen suit. The differences between them seemed all the more apparent because Cass was so conscious of her tear-swollen eyes and pillow-tumbled hair. She was totally unaware of how sensually appealing she looked, but Valerie wasn't.

'You've been away,' she said now, as Cass closed the door behind her. 'For several weeks.'

'Yes.' Cass managed to answer her. 'I suppose Roger told you.'

Valerie hesitated. 'Not exactly.'

Cass's brows drew together. 'But I thought...' She took a steadying breath and struggled to keep calm. 'Look, did you mean what you said just now?'

'About my being married to Roger?' For an answer, Valerie extended her left hand so that Cass could see the thick gold wedding ring that spanned her third finger. 'I don't lie, Mrs—*Miss* Scorcese.'

Cass shook her head. 'But I don't understand. Why are you telling me this? Why *now*?'

Valerie glanced behind her. 'Can I sit down?'

'Oh, of course.' Cass gestured automatically. 'Um—do you want a drink or something? I don't know what we have.'

'Nothing, thanks.' Valerie's response was dry. 'I didn't come here to socialise.'

'Then why did you—'

'I'm coming to that.' Valerie subsided on to the couch and crossed her legs. 'Roger never told you about me, did he?'

Cass moved away from the door, twisting her hands together. 'He didn't have to. I—I saw you together once, in a restaurant. After that, it was easy to guess what he was doing.'

'Ah.' Valerie nodded. 'And was that fairly recently?'

'No.'

'No?'

'No, it was over two years ago, actually.'

'What?' Valerie looked so staggered, Cass had to repeat herself.

'It was about eighteen months after we got married,' she explained. 'I saw you together in Orlando's.' She bent her head. 'It was obvious what was going on. I know Roger's way of—well, of doing things.'

Valerie shook her head. 'The bastard!'

'Why?' Cass blinked. 'Surely you knew he was—he had married me.'

'Oh, yes, I knew that.' Valerie's expression was bitter now. 'I even agreed to the marriage, fool that I was!'

Cass sought a chair now, her legs decidedly unsteady. 'But—how?'

Valerie sighed. 'Roger married me in secret, you see. I—well, to be frank, I didn't have the right connections. His father was still alive at that time, and the old man would have had a fit if he'd known his precious son was chasing a pub landlord's daughter.' She sneered. 'As if it mattered. The old fool only used his army rank because he didn't have a penny to his name. Colonel Hartley Fielding: bankrupt!'

Cass shook her head. 'I never met him.'

'No. He died about fifteen months after we got married. That was when Roger discovered how broke he was. He was pretty mad about it, I can tell you.'

'But his home—his father's house in Gloucestershire?' Roger had told her about that.

'Mortgaged to the hilt,' responded Valerie flatly. 'There was barely enough to pay for the funeral. It was quite a shock, believe me.'

Cass frowned. 'But Roger had a job. He—he was already working for my father.'

'Oh, yes.' Valerie was laconic. 'But Roger likes the good things in life: his handmade shirts and shoes, the very best champagne—oh, and an expensive car. That's absolutely essential.'

Cass gulped. 'And—and you were living with him then?'

'Where else? Oh, not that any of his friends knew that we were married. Until his father died, he had insisted on keeping that quiet. Then, after he was dead, he had other reasons for doing so.'

Cass stared at her disbelievingly. 'Me!'

Valerie had the grace to avoid her eyes. 'Yes.'

Cass tried to think. 'But, you—you can't have approved of what he was doing?'

'Why not?' Valerie lifted her head again. 'I like the good things in life, too. Oh, you wouldn't understand. Never having had to scrape and save for anything in your life. But me, I was hungry for that kind of existence. And Roger can be very persuasive. Very persuasive indeed.'

Cass couldn't take it in. 'But why didn't you divorce him?'

'And let him marry you, free and clear?' Valerie uttered a short, mirthless laugh. 'Oh, no! I wasn't having that. So long as I knew he was married to me, there was no way he could double-cross me. Roger may be charming in some ways, but in others he's quite ruthless.' Cass could believe that. 'We made—an arrangement. He'd marry you, make a lot of money, and then get a divorce, when the time was right.'

Cass gasped. 'I don't believe it!' Yet didn't it explain Roger's swift proposal? His insistence that he wanted to do the right thing? *The right thing!*

'Oh, believe it. It's true.' Valerie fumbled in her bag and brought out a vellum envelope. 'Here. This is our marriage certificate. It's never been revoked. I told you, I don't tell lies.'

'How can you say that when—'

'I haven't lied to you.' Valerie was adamant. 'I haven't betrayed Roger's lies—until now—that's true, but I've never actually endorsed them, have I?'

'But that still doesn't explain why suddenly—'

'I'll tell you.' Valerie bit her lip. 'For the past six months, I've been asking him to leave you. Your marriage was never intended to last more than a year or two, three at most. I never dreamt that your father would practically adopt Roger as his successor, or that Roger would get to like being Guido Scorcese's son-in-law. Call me a fool, if you like, but I thought Roger loved me. I thought nothing could ever come between us. How wrong I was!'

Cass hesitated. 'You didn't know I knew about you—about your—*affair*—with—with my husband?'

'Of course not.' Valerie groaned. 'Roger always used to say that that was how he'd get out of the marriage. That if you ever found out, he would leave you. When *you* say that you've known for—what was it?—more than two years? Why haven't you left him? Didn't you care that he was sleeping with someone else?'

Cass sighed. 'It's a long story. Briefly, I suppose, our marriage wasn't working. I should never have married him. I—well, there was someone else, but...' She broke off for a moment, and then went on, 'So I told my father what was going on.'

'You told your father?' Valerie was amazed. 'But didn't he—'

Cass lifted her shoulders. 'He talked to Roger.'

'He *talked* to Roger?'

'Yes.' Cass coloured. 'He persuaded him that he was being foolish. Roger agreed.'

'I bet he did.' Valerie's face was contorted. 'The rotten sod!' she swore angrily. 'And all the time he pretended you knew nothing about us.'

Cass drew a trembling breath. 'That still doesn't explain what you're doing here now.'

'Oh, no.' Valerie ran unsteady fingers over her forehead, and for the first time Cass felt sorry for her. She was married to Roger; Cass was not—although the true extent of that extraordinary revelation had still to be explored. 'It was your going away, you see. Leaving Roger for almost six weeks. It was obvious that something was wrong. I knew Roger so well. I could tell. Not that he confided in me. As a matter of fact, I haven't seen him for almost a month.'

'You haven't?'

'No.' Valerie's shoulders sagged. 'And then, this afternoon, he phoned me to tell me he wasn't going to see me any more.'

Cass's eyes widened. 'I see.'

'He said you were back in England. He said you'd been ill while you were away, and that was why you'd stayed in Italy so long. He said as soon as you had had time to recover, he was going to take you on a second honeymoon.'

'Oh!' Cass felt utterly amazed. It was like hearing about someone else; not herself at all.

'Anyway,' went on Valerie, 'I knew something had to be done. Roger was so sure I would never betray him, and perhaps I wouldn't have if I hadn't had another reason for doing so. After all, he's been very kind to me over the years. Where do you think this Calvin Klein suit came from, or these Charles Jourdan shoes?'

Cass shook her head. 'I don't think I understand.'

'Don't you?' Valerie's lips twisted. 'Well, I'm pregnant, Miss Scorcese. I'm going to have a baby. Roger's baby. And I'm damned if my son or daughter is going to be dubbed someone else's bastard!'

'But how did she know where you were?' protested Maggie, some hours later, as she and Cass discussed Valerie's visit over another mug of cocoa.

'Oh, she had gone to Knightsbridge to confront Roger—and me, I suppose—but Roger was just leaving. She saw him driving off, and followed him to Eaton Chare. Then she saw me arrive, and I think she became suspicious. Anyway, when I left, she followed me and spent the time it took me to get undressed and go to bed tracing which apartment I'd entered. Luckily, there were only six to choose from.'

Maggie looked absolutely amazed. 'To think Roger was married to her all the time you were living together. You read about these things happening, but you never actually believe it could happen to you. You know what this means, don't you? You're a free woman again! You can do what you like. Your father can't stop you now, can he?'

CHAPTER FOURTEEN

BUT it wasn't her father who troubled Cass in the days that followed. In spite of what had happened, she couldn't quite believe that Roger would let her get away, without doing the thing he had threatened in the library at her parents' home. Every day she expected to wake up to television reports of the 'unnatural relationship' between herself and Ben, and when there were none she went out and bought every tabloid newspaper that might, conceivably, carry such a lurid story. Maggie got tired of filling her dustbin with discarded newsprint, and as she didn't know what her friend was looking for she regarded the whole operation with some suspicion.

From her parents, Cass heard surprisingly little. She had phoned Diana the morning after Valerie Jordan's—no, *Fielding's*—visit, and explained what had happened to her, but Diana had been distinctly unsympathetic.

'The girl's obviously unbalanced,' she exclaimed, dismissing what she had heard without hesitation. 'Roger may have had some relationship with her, I'm not denying that, but don't go condemning him now without any proof.'

'But she had her marriage certificate,' persisted Cass.

'Did you read it?'

'Well—no.'

'There you are, then.' Her mother was triumphant.

'Even so…'

Cass couldn't quite believe that anyone would humiliate themselves as Valerie had without good reason.

'Well, leave it with me,' declared Diana impatiently, the less salubrious aspects of what this might mean if there was a public scandal putting an edge to her voice. 'I'll talk to your father. He'll get to the bottom of it.'

And for the past three days Cass had waited expectantly for her father to appear. She had been quite prepared for him to come storming into Maggie's apartment, insisting that she return to Eaton Chare at once, but he hadn't even returned her call. There had been an ominous silence from all quarters, and Cass was rapidly coming to the uneasy conclusion that it had been a dreadful hoax.

Yet, she argued, in her more optimistic moments, why hadn't Roger contacted her? Why hadn't he pursued his intention to get in touch with her the following day? It was all distinctly unnerving, and she didn't know what she should do.

Maggie was leaving for her holiday in the United States at the end of the week, and Cass knew she was concerned about her lack of contact with her family. 'Why don't you phone your mother again?' Maggie suggested on Thursday evening, two days before she was leaving. 'She must know something. Roger's bound to have seen your father. Don't you think you should make some effort on your own behalf? Who knows what lies Roger's been telling?'

'Maybe.' But Cass was unenthusiastic. She was still half afraid that if she contacted her mother Diana would tell her it had all been a ghastly mistake. So long as she didn't know anything for certain, she could exist in a mindless state of limbo.

Then, on Friday morning, as she was walking back from the local supermarket after buying some bread, a sleek blue Bentley cruised to a stop beside her. Even without the unmistakable sight of George Fisher, her father's chauffeur, at the wheel, she could have recognised the car.

And when the rear window glided open and her father's head appeared she guessed that the waiting was all over.

'Get in, Cass,' he said, thrusting open the door. 'Hurry up. We are not supposed to stop on yellow lines.'

'Since when has that bothered you?' murmured Cass ruefully, but she did as he had suggested and climbed into the comfortable limousine.

Guido Scorcese looked at her silently for a moment, and Cass wondered if he was deploring her tight jeans and crumpled shirt. But then, with a muffled oath he gathered her into his arms, and she knew that, whatever Roger had said, her father had not condemned her out of hand.

'*Cara, cara!*' he exclaimed after a moment, holding her away from him so that he could look into her face. He spoke English usually, without a trace of an accent. But in moments of stress he liked to revert to his native tongue. And right now he was evidently relieved to see her, his eyes holding none of the censure she had expected.

Cass straightened and pushed back her hair behind her ears. 'Have you been to the apartment?'

'I tried there first,' agreed her father, leaning forward to direct Fisher to drive round the park until further notice. Then, pressing the button that raised the glass screen between the chauffeur and themselves, he leaned back again, beside her, studying her so intently that Cass felt her colour deepen.

'So,' he continued, after a moment, 'how are you? Have you seen a doctor since you got back? I asked your mother if you had seen Guthrie but, of course, she had not asked you.'

'I haven't,' said Cass quickly, wishing they could dispense with the formalities. 'Have—have you seen Roger? Did Mummy tell you what—what's going on?'

'Presently, presently.' Guido could be so frustrating when he chose. 'You still haven't told me that you have completely recovered. That was a worrying time for all of us, *cara*. We love you very much, though perhaps we don't always show it.'

'I know you do, Daddy.' Cass endeavoured to control her aggravation. 'And I'm quite well, thank you. Sophia—Signora Scorcese, that is—was very kind. I—I must write and thank her, after—after...'

'After the dust has settled, hmm?' suggested her father drily, and Cass flushed again at the unknowing connotation.

'So you have seen Roger,' she prompted, eager to advance the conversation, and after a moment Guido nodded.

'I've seen him.'

'Well, what did he say? Does he deny it? Oh, Daddy, you've got to tell me what's going on. I can't bear the suspense any longer.'

Her father hesitated. Then he said quietly, 'It's true. How could he deny it? The first thing I did was have my lawyers get a copy of the marriage certificate. There was no mistake. Valerie Jordan is Valerie Fielding.'

'Oh!' Cass breathed a sigh of such relief, she felt as if she had caved in a little inside. 'Oh, I can't believe it!' Then, 'But isn't this going to cause you a lot of embarrassment? Oh—and Mummy's going to be so furious about the scandal!'

'Never mind about your mother,' remarked Guido flatly. 'She'll get over it. We're leaving for Bermuda in a couple of weeks. By the time we get back, the worst of the publicity will have blown over.'

Cass quivered. 'But what about Roger?' Her mouth was dry. 'Isn't what he did illegal?'

'It is.' Guido acknowledged the fact. 'But I suggest you try and forget about Roger, and what might happen to him. He is my concern from now on. You will never see him again.'

Cass licked her lips. 'He may be—vindictive.'

'Yes.' Guido's smile was strangely smug. 'But I think I can handle him. I've done it before.'

'Yes, but…'

'It's not a problem, *cara*.' He shook his head. 'Believe me, you need have no further anxieties on that score. My only regret is that I allowed this to happen, and then endorsed it by believing his lies.'

Cass shook her head. 'I believed him, too.'

'Yes, well…' Her father heaved a sigh. 'Let us put the existence of Roger Fielding behind us for the moment. You and I, *cara*, have more important matters to consider.'

'We do?' Cass frowned, and then she realised what he meant. 'Where I'm going to live, you mean?'

'Not where you are going to live, no,' retorted Guido, shaking his head. 'Does it not surprise you that I have not contacted you for almost a week? After such an earth-shattering revelation, did you not expect me to be hammering on your door the next day?'

'Well…' Cass had to be honest. 'I did wonder why you hadn't rung.'

'Ah.' Guido nodded. 'So, I will tell you why I did not. I could not come to see you, because I was in Italy.'

'Italy?' Cass's colour receded. 'You went to see Ben?' She thought she could guess why, and her stomach muscles clenched.

'No. I went to see Sophia,' her father contradicted her evenly. 'I thought perhaps it was time we—buried the hammer, as they say here.'

'Hatchet,' said Cass automatically. And then, 'Roger told you, didn't he?' Her heart was palpitating. 'He told you that Ben and I—that we—' She choked. 'But there's something you don't know—'

'Gently, *cara*, gently.' Overcoming her instinctive resistance, Guido gathered her into his arms again, and held her close. 'All right, all right. Yes, Roger did make his futile accusations, but they were never more than that. *Cara*, I've always known that Benvenuto was not my natural offspring. What, do you think your father is a fool? But, believe it or not, I was madly in love with Sophia in those days, and I was prepared to take her, pregnant or otherwise.'

Cass could only stare at him. 'But—but why—'

'Why didn't I tell her?' Guido shrugged. 'How could I? She was so proud of her deception. And Ben is my son. In everything but blood.'

'But when Ben found out—'

'He didn't tell me. How could he? But I guessed he knew.' Guido paused, and then went on, 'The summer he graduated, with a first in history and economics, he went home to see his mother. The plan, as you know now, was for him to join the company after his holiday was over. But when he came back, everything had changed. He came to see me, and told me he wanted to stay at college. He said he had decided to take a doctorate in medieval studies instead of opting for commerce.'

'Oh, Daddy!' Cass could imagine how her father must have felt.

'Yes. As you obviously understand, I was furious. But, short of telling him the truth, there was nothing I could do. I was sure Sophia would not have told him, and when I telephoned her at Calvado, it was obvious she was upset

by his decision. But someone must have said something—'

'His grandmother,' murmured Cass unsteadily, and
Guido sighed.

'Ah.' He nodded. 'I should have guessed. She never
approved of our marriage.'

'Why not?'

'Oh…' Guido shrugged. 'I was not one of them. My
father owned land in the valley, but he was never there.
He preferred Genoa, and only when I was on holiday from
school, or later from university, was I allowed to go and
work alongside them.'

'I see.' Cass nodded. 'And you—fell in love with Sophia.'

'That's right.' Guido was rueful. 'She was—is still—a
beautiful woman. And when Francesco was so tragically
killed, I took advantage of her weakness.'

Cass was trying hard to take this in, but still there were
questions to be answered. 'So why did you go and see
Sophia?' she breathed.

'Why do you think?'

'Roger?' Cass's voice was very low.

'Roger,' agreed Guido softly. 'But you know, he did
us all a favour.'

'He did?'

'Of course. He made me see what a fool I had been all
these years.' Guido sighed again. 'Do you remember
when you used to spend your summers at Calvado?' Cass
nodded, not trusting herself to speak, and he continued, 'I
always believed you were the key to the solution. Ben
was fond of you. I knew that. It was because of you he
stayed and took his doctorate in London. I suppose I
hoped that one day he might confide in you. I even

thought how wonderful it would be if you two fell in love.'

'Daddy!'

'Oh, I know. He is a few years older than you are, but you always seemed to prefer his company to anyone else's. Your mother was very jealous, I can tell you. And not just because *you* preferred Ben.'

Cass was shaking. 'But I thought he was my *brother*!'

'Yes, I realise that now.' Guido groaned. 'Sophia told me what happened that summer at Calvado. You would never have become involved with Roger if I had not been so obtuse.'

Cass moved away from him, needing time to get things into perspective. He was going too fast for her now. Where before her questions had jumped ahead of him, now she was confused by so many conflicting answers.

'So—so,' she stammered at last, 'are you now going to tell everyone that—that Ben is not your son?'

'No.'

'No?' Cass almost choked on the word.

'No.' Guido put his hand beneath her chin and tilted her face to his. 'I shall simply explain, to those who need to know, that Ben is my adopted son. That his father was killed before he was born, and that naturally I have always regarded him as mine.'

'Oh, Daddy!'

Guido's face gentled. 'Does that please you?'

Cass nodded. 'You must know it does.'

'I don't *know* anything,' retorted Guido flatly. 'Except some garbled story Fielding was flinging around about you and Ben having a—how did he put it?—a relationship.'

Cass's lips trembled. 'You haven't seen Ben, then?'

'No.' Guido hesitated. 'I wanted to see you first.' He

gave her a wry look. 'But now, I think perhaps I should have done.'

'No.' Cass made a negative gesture. 'No, let me tell Ben. Unless his mother's already done so...'

'She hasn't,' declared Guido firmly. 'Believe me, you may still have some trouble from that quarter. She's not at all convinced that my daughter is good enough for *her* son!'

'Oh, Daddy!'

Cass flung herself into his arms then, laughing and crying and talking all at once. When she'd woken up this morning her state of limbo had seemed the best she could hope for. Now she had much higher aspirations. And a desperate need to put them into practice.

She hired a car at the airport in Pisa, and drove herself the eighty or so kilometres between there and Florence. The traffic was heavy on the *autostrada*. It was, after all, one of the peak weekends of the holiday season, and Cass had only got a seat on the plane at all because of her father's influence.

Florence itself was jammed with cars and buses, full of tourists eager to sample the cultural delights of the city. To Cass, who was eager to reach her destination, the cheerful hoots and honking of horns was simply a frustration, and gave her too much time to worry about what she would do if Ben had gone away.

It was late afternoon before she turned into the Piazza del Fiore, and parked the borrowed Lancia in front of Ben's apartment building. There was a sign which she thought meant 'No Parking', but she decided to worry about that only if she had to. For the moment, she was more intent on checking out Ben's windows. They were open, but that could be because Mrs Cipriani was doing her cleaning. She had come here so many times before and found him absent that she couldn't believe this time he'd be at home.

She climbed the stairs too fast, and by the time she reached Ben's landing her head was spinning. That was when she remembered she'd had nothing but drinks all day. She'd refused to eat anything on the plane, and since she'd landed she hadn't thought about food.

The doorbell seemed to echo in the hall long after she had pressed the button. Was that because the apartment was empty? she wondered anxiously. Wouldn't Ben have come to answer it if he was here?

She pressed it again, a little ache beginning in her temple at the thought that Ben might have gone to Calvado. Or if not there, some other place; or even out of the country. Dear heaven, she couldn't bear the thought that it might be *days* before she could reach him. Weeks, even, if he hadn't left a forwarding address. With the university closed, and no idea how to reach any of his colleagues, what could she do?

When the door abruptly opened, she almost collapsed with relief. But the young woman who was standing facing her was totally unfamiliar, and the sickly sense of desperation returned to clutch her stomach.

'*Sì?*' The girl, Cass guessed she was about nineteen, surveyed the visitor without enthusiasm. '*Posso aiutarla?*'

Cass was struggling with the devastating realisation that this girl must be some friend of Ben's. For a moment, the girl's words didn't even mean anything to her. She could hardly think in English, let alone in Italian.

The girl sighed. '*Che cosa desidera?*' she exclaimed, clearly growing impatient with Cass's apparent stupidity. '*Capisce?*' She frowned. '*Parla Italiano?*'

'*Un po,*' murmured Cass at last, finding a suitable answer. 'A little,' and the girl nodded.

'You are English,' she declared, with a pronounced, if
faintly patronising, accent. '*Bene*, can I help you? Do you
wish to speak with Professore Scorcese?'

'Professore Scorcese?' echoed Cass faintly, realising
she had never heard his academic title used before. And,
although she was strongly tempted to get out of here while
she still retained a little self-respect, she nodded. 'Yes.
Yes, I would like to speak to—to Signor Scorcese. Is—is
he at home?'

'Francesca!'

The sound of Ben's voice silenced both of them for a
moment, and Cass's knees shook inside her dark blue cotton flying suit as his footsteps sounded along the hall.
Even now she had a cowardly urge to turn tail and run.
But the need to see him again was stronger than her fears,
and in spite of the girl's presence she remained where she
was.

Then, when Ben appeared out of the shadows of the
hall, her heart almost stopped beating. He looked so *pale*!
All the natural colour seemed to have drained out of his
face, and there were dark circles around his eyes and a
growth of stubble on his chin.

'Francesca,' he said again, looking at the girl. '*Cos'e?*'
Then he saw Cass.

'Someone for you, Zio Benvenuto,' declared Francesca
confidently, clearly unaware of any undercurrents at
that moment. '*E*—you did not give me your name,
signora— '

'It's Cass,' said Ben harshly, interrupting her. He was
staring at Cass with unbelieving eyes. 'Um...' He raked
back his hair with a hand that she saw was rather unsteady. 'Look,' he spoke to the girl beside him in rapid

Italian, 'do you mind if we abandon our studies for today, Francesca? This—this is an old friend from England, and—we'd like to be alone.'

'Oh, really—' began Cass, but Ben's look silenced her, and as it did so she remembered what Francesca had called him. *Zio!* Uncle! She had called Ben Uncle Benvenuto. Not some girlfriend, then, but obviously a relative. Cass could have almost cried with relief.

'All right.' Francesca didn't look altogether delighted at the interruption, but evidently Ben's word was law. 'I'll just get my books,' she added, darting back down the hall to the living-room, and while she did so Ben invited Cass in.

'What a surprise,' he said, speaking her language now, trying, Cass could tell, to recover his lost composure. For a few moments there, he had looked at her as if he was hungry for the sight of her. But he had himself in control again, and now his eyes were guarded.

'Yes, isn't it?' murmured Cass in reply as Francesca passed them on her way to the door.

'Can I come back again tomorrow?' she asked, her eyes on Cass, frankly curious.

'I'll ring you,' Ben replied, clearly non-committal.

Francesca muttered, *'Ciao!'* rather sulkily as she let herself out of the door.

The living-room was so familiar, Cass wanted to fling herself down on to the sofa, and beg Ben to join her. But Francesca's appearance had taken the edge off her confidence, and for the first time she wondered what she would do if Ben had changed his mind about her.

'My—cousin Victor's daughter,' Ben murmured, by way of an explanation for Francesca's presence. 'She's taking a degree in English Studies. I offered to give her some tuition.'

Cass nodded. 'I see.'

Ben nodded, too, almost absently. And then, running a hand over the growth of beard that roughened his jawline, he said, 'I'm afraid I wasn't expecting company. I must look grim!' He moved over to his desk and shuffled a pile of papers into order. 'I'll get rid of these, and then I'll go and have a shower. Oh—' He turned. 'Can I offer you a drink?'

'I've been drinking all day,' murmured Cass, and then, realising how that might sound, she grimaced. 'I mean, tea, coffee, soft drinks and so on. Not the hard stuff. Not any longer.'

'Good for you.' But Ben's lips twisted a little as he said it. 'I—regrettably—can't say the same. In fact, that's exactly what I need now.'

'Oh, Ben!' For the first time, Cass let her emotions show in her voice. 'You look awful! What have you been doing to yourself?'

'I've just told you,' he retorted, straightening from the desk, and running the palm of one hand down the seam of the worn jeans he was wearing, 'I wasn't expecting visitors. If I'd known you were coming...'

'Shaving isn't going to make much difference,' exclaimed Cass unsteadily. 'Oh, Ben! You have missed me, haven't you?'

His fists balled. 'Why have you come here, Cass?' he demanded tiredly. 'I thought we'd said all we had to say to one another.'

Cass linked her fingers together. 'Just—just answer the question, Ben,' she responded. 'Just for me. *Please!*'

'Don't be a fool!' he muttered, walking wearily towards the door. 'I'm going to take a shower and get a drink, not necessarily in that order. If you can't think of anything more intelligent to say, then I suggest you get out of here before I come back. I'm not really in the mood to be sociable.'

Cass sighed. 'Is that what you really want?' she asked.

'Yes. *No!* Oh, for heaven's sake, Cass, what do you want me to say? Yes. Yes, I have missed you. There, are you satisfied?'

Cass caught her breath. 'Ben—'

'What? Do you want more?' He turned at the door, his face grim with misery. 'All right, I'll give you more. It's killing me; does that please you? The idea that you and Fielding might be back together again is tearing me apart. What did you think it would do? *Please me?*'

Cass shook her head, her eyes glazed with tears. 'Roger—Roger and I are not getting back together,' she told him, with the carefully enunciated words of a witness. 'I never want to see Roger again.'

'That makes two of us,' muttered Ben harshly. 'OK.' He threaded his fingers through his hair once again and nodded. 'OK. We'll talk,' he promised. 'But—but not until I've got rid of this.' His hand slid down to his jawline.

'All right.'

Blinking back her tears, Cass acknowledged his acquiescence, and with a sudden compression of his lips Ben went out of the room. Presently, she heard the sound of the taps running in the bathroom and, unable to stay still even for a minute, she followed him out into the hall. But instead of turning towards the bedroom she turned into the kitchen instead, catching her breath at the pile of dishes lying unwashed in the sink.

It was so unlike Ben to leave the place in such disorder that she went out of the kitchen again, and along the passage to his bedroom. The sound of the running water was much stronger in here, and she looked about her for a moment before walking tremulously across to the bathroom door.

The door was ajar, and the noise of the shower drowned out the sound of her approach. She hesitated just a moment, and then the temptation to be with him overwhelmed her inhibitions. With shaking fingers, she unbuttoned the flying suit and slipped it off. Then she swept off the silk panties, which were all she had been wearing underneath, and stepped into the room.

The door to the shower cubicle was closed, and Ben had his back to her. It was a comparatively simple exercise to open the door and step inside, but when she moved close to him and slid her arms around his waist from behind, he shuddered uncontrollably.

'Hell, Cass!' he groaned, turning in her arms, and obviously intent on getting her out of there, but Cass was ready for him.

'Daddy knows,' she said simply, winding her arms around his neck and pressing herself close to the lean strength of his thighs. 'Hmm, Ben, don't talk. Just love me!'

Whether Ben truly understood her at that moment was debatable, but the moist warmth of her tongue darting between his lips was too great an enticement. His mouth opened on hers, his tongue plunging intimately into that dark, sweet cavern, and Cass felt his growing hardness against her stomach as his hands curved over her bottom.

They were on fire for one another, and each kiss was more sensual than the one before, until at last Ben lifted her to meet his swollen need, and she wound her legs around him in sexual abandon.

With the water still bathing their sweating bodies, it was a shamelessly erotic experience, and Cass cried when at last he lowered her to the tiled floor. 'I love you, I love you,' she breathed, covering his damp chest with kisses, and then, taking the soap from its dish, she began to massage his body with innocently exploring hands.

'Do you have any idea what you're doing?' Ben demanded unsteadily, his need for her seemingly endless.

'I think so,' she murmured, tilting her face up to his before continuing her massage, and when his masculinity filled her hands she bent to kiss him.

'Cass,' he choked, snatching the soap from her hands, and then, swinging her up into his arms, he carried her out of the bathroom and into his bedroom.

'The covers,' she protested, as he lowered her on to the bedspread, but he was already coming down on top of her.

'They'll dry,' he said huskily, burying his face between her breasts. 'Hmm, you taste wonderful!'

'So do you,' she told him unevenly, as his tongue probed one button-hard nipple. 'Oh, Ben, do it! Do it again! Do it now!'

It was over an hour—and a bottle of Chianti—later, that Cass was able to describe the events of the past two weeks in more detail. They had made love and slept and made love again, before she could rouse herself sufficiently to explain the whole story. But when she did Ben was naturally staggered.

'So you're not married to Roger? You've never been married to him?' he exclaimed yet again, and she sighed.

'No.'

'Dear heaven!' Ben, who was propped on his elbow beside her, bent to cover her lips with his. 'When I think of all the energy I've expended on that bastard!'

'What energy?' Cass was intrigued.

'Well,' Ben's tongue stroked the contours of her ear, 'I

have to admit, I have spent sleepless nights planning ways of getting rid of him. The Borgias had some very original methods.'

Cass's lips parted. 'You were jealous.'

'No.' She pouted, and he smiled. 'Paranoid,' he amended drily. 'You have no idea of the torment you've put me though.'

'Haven't I?' Cass touched his cheek. 'I wouldn't be too sure about that, if I were you—'

Ben stopped her protest with his mouth, and for several minutes there was silence in the apartment. Then he said unsteadily, 'So, tell me again about your father.'

'What about him?' Cass was drowsy now.

'You mean, he knew I wasn't his son when he wanted me to go and work for him?'

'Mmm.' Cass burrowed against him. 'He still regards you as his son. After all, it's the person who brings someone up who's their real father. Except biologically, of course.'

'Thank heaven for that!' said Ben fervently, gathering her into his arms. 'I wonder what my mother really said.'

'Daddy said we might still have some trouble from that quarter.'

'Nothing I can't handle,' declared Ben firmly, confident now. And then, 'Are you hungry?'

'Only for you,' said Cass simply, and he couldn't argue with that.

They were married two months later, in London, despite Sophia's objections that they ought to have taken their vows at the church in Calvado. Still, as that had been her only voiced objection, Ben and Cass weren't too worried. The fact that Cass was already six weeks pregnant at the time of the wedding might have had something to do with it. Sophia was quite excited at the prospect of becoming a grandmother herself at last.

The delay before the wedding had been to allow the Press coverage concerning Roger's disclosed bigamy to subside, though there were still journalists willing to couple the two events in their front-page stories. However, Cass and Ben's happiness was unmistakable, and Guido made sure no journalist gatecrashed the private party the family held afterwards.

Roger himself seemed to have disappeared. Certainly he had never been arrested for his crime, and Ben guessed Guido had had something to do with that, too. Without the leading protagonist, the story was infinitely less newsworthy, and Ben no longer felt any real animosity towards the man who had tried so hard to keep his secret. They had all had secrets, Ben reflected wryly. Not least himself.

For his part, he felt he must be the happiest man alive. He had loved Cass for so long, and now she was his. And, what was more, she had declared her intention to become the perfect academic's wife.

'You do realise your father is expecting me to change my mind about joining the company now?' he asked her one morning, about a week after the wedding, coming into the bedroom of their honeymoon suite in Hawaii, and finding his wife sitting naked in the middle of the sheets. She was munching shamelessly through the tray of croissants he had had delivered earlier, and she looked up at him mischievously, wiping a smear of butter from her lips.

'I hope you're not hungry,' she said, as he wrapped a towel about his hips and sank down beside her. 'Have some coffee. It's delicious! It's almost as good as ours. Are you looking forward to getting back home?'

Ben regarded her with unconcealed emotion, his eyes dark with the passion she could so effortlessly set alight.

'Home,' he said softly. 'Are you sure you want to go back to Italy? We can buy a bigger house, of course, but is being a professor's wife going to satisfy you? I mean...' He sighed. 'It's going to be very different from living in London.'

'I hope so,' said Cass fervently, putting the tray aside, and leaning back against him. 'Mmm...' She sighed contentedly as his hand closed round her breast. 'Can we talk about this later? We have better things to do right now.'

'No, we don't,' said Ben firmly, propelling her away from him, and looking at her with earnest eyes. 'Is that really what you want? Or would you rather I changed my mind?'

'I want to do what you want,' said Cass steadily. 'And you want to stay a teacher, don't you?'

'Well...'

'You see.' Cass was triumphant. 'Don't worry about Daddy. He'll have a grandson soon to inherit his money. He's not old. It'll be years before he retires, and when he does, we'll think about it then.'

Ben pulled her close. 'You're sure?'

'I'm sure.'

'I love you.'

'I hope so.' She dimpled. 'Now, are you going to make love to me or not?'

Ben groaned. 'In your condition—'

'In my condition, I'm very sexy,' declared Cass happily, falling back against the silk sheets and taking him with her. 'Hmm, this towel's wet. You don't need it, do you? Oh, no, that's much better. Don't you agree?'

And he did.

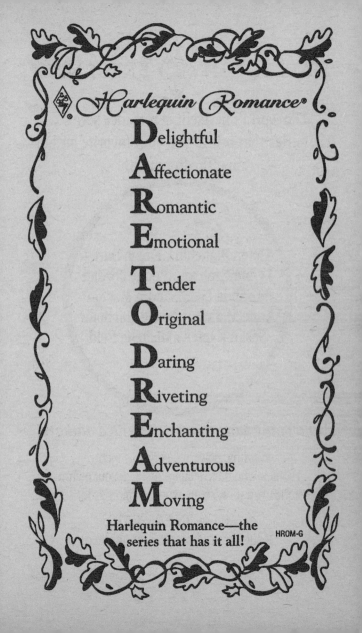

Harlequin Romance®

Delightful

Affectionate

Romantic

Emotional

Tender

Original

Daring

Riveting

Enchanting

Adventurous

Moving

Harlequin Romance—the
series that has it all!

HROM-G

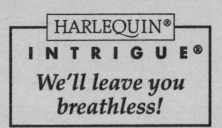

Harlequin®
Historical

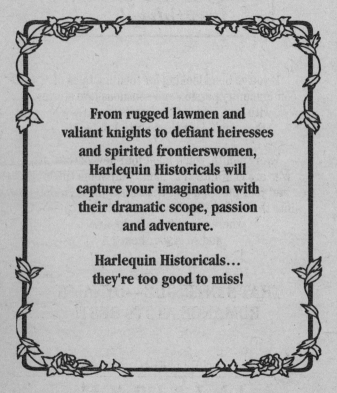

From rugged lawmen and
valiant knights to defiant heiresses
and spirited frontierswomen,
Harlequin Historicals will
capture your imagination with
their dramatic scope, passion
and adventure.

Harlequin Historicals…
they're too good to miss!

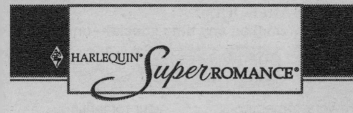

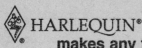